© Ibadan University Press, Publishing House, University of Ibadan, Ibadan, Nigeria

First published in 2024

ISBN: 978-978-8550-28-0

Chapter One

Mudiaga is Born Physically Disabled

"Congratulations again, Mama Ese. You've given birth to a big bouncing black baby boy," Matron Etobo informed Esama for the second time. Esama was delivered about an hour ago at the *God Saves Maternity & Nursing Home* in Ogonbiri community. About five minutes after the delivery, Esama was sweating profusely, in pain, and still in a drowsy and debilitating state when she was informed for the first time that she had delivered a baby boy. At 11:00 p.m, after Esama and her baby boy had been cleaned up, they were both taken to the single-room maternity ward containing four beds.

"Thank you, God," Esama supplicated while lying face up on the bed. "I now have a girl and a boy without any complications in their bodies. Papa Ese will be very happy now that he has a boy omomo."

Esama recollected that her husband had escorted her to the maternity nursing home when she was having frequent contractions and tightenings, but she had not seen him since her delivery of the baby. She asked the matron, "Matron, where is my husband, sef?"

"Immediately after you delivered, your husband peeped into the labour room and asked, 'What type of child did my wife give birth to?' I told him, 'A bulky boy.' He ran outside and shouted, 'I'm now a papa of a boy! My name will not be lost when I die!' Then, he vanished into the darkness outside," Matron Etobo informed Esama.

"My husband really wanted me to give birth to a boy," Esama observed. "He will go and drink *ogogoro* and peppersoup at *People's Bar* with his *yeye* friends tonight."

"Yes, indeed! A boy child is considered gold in the Ogonbiri community and all communities in Olobiri state," responded Matron Etobo.

"I don't want to have another child. I now have two children without any complications. I'm afraid. I don't want to give birth to a child with complications," stated Esama with a hearty laughter. By"But, Mama Ese, this big baby boy of yours has a small complication," stated Matron Etobo. She paused and then added, "His left leg is bent backward from his knee to his ankle."

"What do you mean? What is *anukul*?" Esama asked in a despondent tone with a frown on her face.

"It's the part of the leg that bends when you kneel down," responded Matron Etobo. She lifted the baby from the bed, unwrapped the swaddle blanket, and showed Esama the naked baby. "Look."

"Hope you didn't switch my child?" Esama asked in a tearful tone. "Switch? No, never!" responded the matron. "Only you delivered here today. Your mother saw it immediately after the baby was born."

"God, why me? And my pastor assured me that the baby was complete in my belly before I delivered it," Esama exclaimed in frustration.

Esama added that her husband had gone to make a sacrifice to their community deity known as Osulu with a goat, and the priest of the deity assured him that the child would not have any complications. Matron Etobo stated that she only knew about the physical disability of the baby boy and that it would take about two years before it would be known if the baby had any form of mental disability, which is usually developmental mental deformity.

'Msssiuuu!' Esama hissed. 'What type of wahala is this? Darkness has enveloped my family.'

Matron Etobo tried to comfort Esama, assuring her that the disabled baby boy she saw as a burden might one day be her most prosperous child. "Shower him with love," she advised. "A child responds to the affection they receive."

"Matron, I'm so confused and sad," Esama confessed, tears welling up in her eyes.

Sweat trickled down Esama's face as a sharp pain returned, intensifying despite previously subsiding. Grimacing, she clutched her head and cried out, "My head!" The sudden headache felt like a spike piercing her skull.

Lost in worry, Esama looked up at the crumbling asbestos ceiling above. A ceiling fan hung in the ward, but due to the unreliable electricity, it rarely spun. When she'd given birth, they'd managed to turn it on briefly, offering some relief from the heat. The locals, however, had a less flattering nickname for it – "Mama Etobo's Caterpillar" – due to its jarring noise. The cost of powering the small generator, nicknamed "I Better Pass My Neighbor," was

added to the hospital bill, further burdening new mothers like Esama. This generator, notorious for its fumes and grating noise, had earned another nickname: "God Saves Maternity's Cassava Grinding Machine." The persistent whine of the generator seemed to amplify the creaking of the old mattress beneath Esama and her newborn.
The discomfort it caused mirrored the turmoil in her mind.

The torn bed sheet, discolored from white to gray, offered little comfort on the worn-out mattress. The flat pillow provided no support for Esama's head. In frustration, she flung it aside. With no crib beside the bed, she was forced to share it with her son. Mosquitoes buzzed relentlessly in the ward, as there were no nets on the termite-eaten windows. The once blue paint on the walls was peeling, revealing a patchy mix of gray and blue.

Esama, a young woman in her early twenties of average height and chocolate complexion, bore the stark reminder of a past tragedy. Seven years ago, she narrowly escaped death when a gas flare cone exploded near Enwen, where women were drying kpokpogarri and fish. The scars – burns on her chin and shoulder – were a constant reminder. She had been about two hundred metres away, walking towards the site to buy some kpokpogarri to sell at Databri market the next day, when the disaster struck.

Esama wondered audibly how her husband would react when he learned of their son's disability. Matron Etobo offered reassurance. She promised that doctors could correct the baby's leg before his second birthday. With a smile, she predicted a brighter future. By the time Esama gave birth again, which the matron was certain would be twins, the maternity ward would be completely renovated. Gone would be the old beds, replaced with new ones adorned with Dunlop mattresses and pillows, fresh bed sheets, and imported cribs for newborns.

"Give birth again after this boy with a twisted leg?" Esama scoffed. "Never! God forbid!" She made a dismissive gesture, swinging her hand over her head three times.

Matron Etobo cautioned Esama against having only two children. She warned that her husband might take another wife if she didn't produce more children, claiming that four was the minimum a woman should have unless she suffered from secondary infertility.
Matron Etobo, a stout, dark-skinned woman in her sixties, bustled about in her blue scrubs. Her gray hair glinted under the dim yellow bulb. Her gait resembled that of a lumbering, seven-month pregnant African elephant. Despite advice to reduce her food intake and exercise to combat obesity-related illnesses like type two diabetes and heart diseases or worse still, stroke, Matron remained averse to change.

For twenty years, she had served as an auxiliary midwife in various Olobiri State health centres before opening her own maternity and nursing home in her hometown. Though her vision was failing, she stubbornly refused to replace the three pairs of medicated glasses she'd lost or broken. Priye, her assistant, had repeatedly advised her to be more careful but to no avail.

When Esama went into labour, the delivery room was illuminated only by a bush lamp. Priye announced that the baby appeared to have "one and a half legs."

"Let me examine him myself," Matron Etobo insisted. After checking the baby, she confirmed, "The baby's leg is bent backward. What youthful eyes miss, experience reveals."

Priye, the midwifery assistant, apologized, "Sorry, Mummy." "A young person may have a closet full of new clothes, but they cannot have more experience than their elders," Matron countered. "Perhaps you see your own disability – impatience – while I see the ability within my failing vision – experience and patience."

Priye, a light-skinned young woman of eighteen who lived with her parents, couldn't help but marvel. "It's like Matron has three eyes," she thought. Priye aspired to become a nurse after she passed her ordinary level exams. Her dream was to work in an oil industry clinic.

Esama confided in the matron that caring for a disabled child felt like caring for triplets. She contemplated abandoning the baby and leaving her husband, despite Peregba's kindness.
Matron Etobo countered, "There are many disabled children in oilrich Olobiri State, but fewer in Ogonbiri because the land lacks crude oil. Don't abandon this innocent child."
Esama, weary, ate two pieces of boiled unripe plantain and peppersoup her mother had brought. Exhausted, she drifted off to sleep.
***

When Peregba joyfully sauntered out of *God Saves Maternity and Nursing Home* the night his wife was delivered of a baby boy, he went to his friend's room where Ese, his daughter, was staying the night. Peregba lifted her from the mat she was sleeping on and he told her:

'Your omomo brother has arrived. Your mama born boy.'
He told his neighbour and good friend the good news.
'Good news,' Orode stated. 'Hope the baby is well and healthy.'
'You can ask mumu question. The boy is very strong,' responded
Peregba. 'The boy health dey kampe. When the boy hala cry, the
roof of the *God saves maternity* almost collapse.'

Orode congratulated his friend on becoming the father of two
healthy children. Peregba explained that a nurse told him in
Olobiri state, typically, if a woman delivers a healthy firstborn, the
second child is also healthy. He added that he performed a
libation to his ancestors and sacrificed a male goat to the
community's Osulu deity. The priest assured him his wife would
deliver a healthy baby. Peregba also accompanied his wife to
Reverend Samson's church, Miraculous Prayers Church, for
prayers. His wife likewise visited two other churches for fasting
and prayers. The couple made generous donations to the
churches.

'I'm happy and jealous of you oo!' noted Orode with a perturbing
smile. He explained that his first son, Uvo, has a complication in
his brain. Uvo is almost four years old and he still cannot talk well.
Matron Etobo told Orode that Uvo has a half human brain and a
lion's power. Orode concluded, saying Matron Etobo
affectionately calls Uvo "Samson".

'Oya o. Let's go and celebrate at *People's Bar*,' Peregba told his
friend with a tone of compassion as he pulled his friend up from
the chair he had been sitting on. Peregba had always supported
his friend after his wife left him following a stillbirth during their
second delivery. Orode was now considering choosing a wife from
one of the three women who were major distributors of
petroleum products from his local, artisanal refinery deep within

the labyrinthine creeks of Enwen Local Government Area in Olobiri State.

At the bar, Peregba bought a small bottle of ogogoro and four plates of fresh fish peppersoup for his friends. He confided in his friend that since his wife was from Enwen, a community with two oil wells, two gas flare cones, and a flow station, he had worried about the possibility of having children with disabilities.

"Thank goodness your wife avoided having children with disabilities," Orode remarked.

"We still want two more children," Peregba declared with a smile. "My wife will always avoid having children with disabilities whenever she gets pregnant."

The friends spent about two hours at the bar before heading home. In the morning, before Peregba left for the maternity home to see his wife and son, Orode gave him two ten-litre jerrycans of kerosene as a gift.

'Thank you, managing director of Orode refinery,' Peregba hailed his friend.

Peregba wondered if he could survive the psychological laceration that Orode had endured for the past five years. Uvo's mother had abandoned her son when he was about a year and a half old, unable to handle raising a child with a developmental disability. Peregba and Orode were both dark-skinned men of average height. Peregba was slender and bearded, while Orode was stocky and bald. They were roughly the same age, in their late twenties. Additionally, Orode had bowed legs and six fingers and toes on each hand and foot. A cobbler made his shoes and sandals, and he usually wore oversized rain boots when working at his local refinery in the maze of creeks.

Peregba's home is a four-room building with a living room. The kitchen, toilet, and bathroom are located in an extension on the left side. The building remains unpainted. Orode rents two of the rooms. He uses one as storage for his refinery supplies. A wooden pedestrian bridge provides access during the rainy season when floods inundate parts of Ogonibiri. December's dry season means the community is currently without flooding. During heavy rains, water submerges about a metre of the buildings in most areas, although raised foundations typically keep the interiors dry. Two small fish ponds sit behind the building, with a river that overflows its banks annually located around two hundred metres further back. Medium-sized fish ponds are a common feature in the community, similar to ornamental gardens elsewhere. Uvo stays with Peregba's family whenever his father travels to the refinery for several days.

In the morning, Peregba's mother-in-law, Mama Obere, arrived to prepare peppersoup and cook unripe plantains for her daughter. Peregba noticed her working diligently, but also sighing and hissing constantly. Despite these signs, she remained silent about the baby's disability, perhaps assuming he already knew. About thirty minutes after Ese and Mama Obere left with the food, Peregba decided to visit his wife and newborn son.

Upon arrival at *God Saves Maternity and Nursing Home*, Peregba noticed his wife's dejection. Though his wife was breastfeeding the baby, no one offered any explanation.

"What's going on?" he blurted out in frustration. "Is the baby boy sick?" He tapped his wife's shoulder for attention.

Our baby has a clubfoot," Esama choked out through tears. She gently unwrapped the worn cloth, revealing their son's twisted left leg to her husband.

"What is this?!" Peregba cried out in shock. He slumped down onto the floor, overwhelmed.

"I feel like a dog eating its own vomit," Peregba fumed. "After bragging about my son being a strong lion, now I have to swallow my pride and tell everyone he has a disability." He spoke with a mix of anger and confusion.

He stood up, cradled the baby in his arms, and said, "Let me just try to straighten the leg."

"Are you trying to hurt the baby?" the matron and Priye responded in unison.
"Why God? Why Osulu? After all the prayers and sacrifices?" Peregba cried out in despair.

He turned to the matron and asked, "Why didn't you tell me yesterday?"

"Did you even wait? You left as soon as I told you the baby's sex."
"Goodness! Why all this sadness and arguing?" Obere wondered. Speaking in proverbs, she said, "Life itself is the greatest gift." Obere added that her grandson's minor deformity shouldn't cause such mourning, as if the baby were dead. She then asked her daughter, "Do you have any idea what the future holds for this boy?"
"If you and Ese don't want the child, let me take him home with me," she offered.

"Taking care of this child will be a real challenge, Mother," Peregba admitted.

"There's no problem at all," the matron reassured the parents. "Bone doctors can correct the baby's leg before he turns four."

Chapter Two

Mudiaga and His Mother at Home

Despite the discovery of their son's clubfoot, Esama and her newborn were discharged from God Saves Maternity and Nursing Home the following day. Obere carried her grandson while Esama and Ese followed closely behind. As they stepped out of the ward, Esama noticed the faded brown paint on the wall of the maternity ward and nursing home, the building, consisting of five rooms and a living room, housed the maternity ward as the last room on the right side. In front of the building stood a raised concrete well, about two feet above the ground. Esama and her mother observed a woman fetching water from the well into a bowl, noting its brownish colour. 'Ogonbiri with coloured water,' Obere muttered audibly. She recalled that the water in her community was cleaner than that of Ogonbiri.

The front of the building was unkempt and there were two long clotheslines strung for drying laundry. The neighbouring houses huddled together like cassava stems in a cassava farm. Since schools were on holidays, children were seen playing in front of the compound. The family members of three generations meandered their way through various compounds till they got to the untarred road that bifurcates the community. The road led southwards to Ona River jetty. The riverbank was always a hub of activities with boats ferrying passengers to other riverine communities while smaller dug-out canoes paddled across the river to access farmlands on the opposite side. Orode's refinery lay further inland, beyond these farms. Northward, the road led to an intersection or a semiroundabout, connecting to other communities. Motorcycles, bicycles and tricycles, locally known as *keke*, frequently plied the road. A lorry laden with planks passed by heading north from Ona River Jetty.

The family members crossed the road and walked for about thirty minutes before they arrived at Peregba's residence. On their way, women, men and children greeted and felicitated with the mother and the newborn baby. They eventually arrived home. News of Esama's delivery spread swiftly throughout the community like wildfire during the harmattan season. Upon arriving home, wellwishers gathered to welcome mother and her newborn baby.

Inside the house, Esama, her mother, the baby and Ese settled into the bedroom, while Peregba arranged an extra mattress in the parlour for himself. The three chairs in the parlour, one three-seater and two single seaters, were lumped together to make space for the mattress. A large mosquito net draped over the big bed to ensure the baby's protection from mosquito bites. Peregba noticed that Ese preferred to spend the night with him in the parlour.

Two weeks after the baby's birth, the Ogonbiri women held a celebration to welcome the newborn and congratulate Esama. During this ceremony, the baby's name was officially announced. A group of community women, traditionally dressed, visited Esama and her baby boy, offering reassurance that orthopaedic surgeons would correct the deformity in his left leg before he grew up.

The women were divided into two groups: the young mothers, dressed in white blouses, yellow wrappers and yellow headties, numbering about fifteen; and the elderly grandmothers, donning brown blouses, blue wrappers and brown headties, totaling around ten. Each guest showcased a unique style of makeup and adorned themselves with variegated jewelry. Esama adorned in a goldcoloured blouse, gold wrapper and elabourate makeup accessorized with beautiful jewelry, matched her husband's outfit. He complemented his outfit with a hat and walking stick. The leader of the grandmothers' delegation was matron Etobo. She walked with the aid of a walking stick. Her left leg is bigger than her right leg, causing a slight limp when she walked. She assured the parents of her commitment to ensuring the baby's leg deformity was corrected by orthopaedic surgeons. Esama's best friend, Eloho, took charge of distributing food and water to the guests. As she wasn't a mother yet, Eloho couldn't wear the white and yellow attire reserved for mothers her age.

Married for four years, Eloho remained childless. Her husband fathered a child with a concubine, who was now pregnant again and living in their home. Constantly taunted for her infertility, Eloho found solace in Esama's company, spending much of her time there. Eloho faced further turmoil when Orode secretly ogled and complimented her whenever they met. Eloho's husband threw out her belongings and refused to share a bed with her due to her infertility. Eloho kept some of her properties in her mother's home and brought some to Esama's home. She now spends more time in Esama's home. With her husband uninterested in the marriage, Eloho contemplated accepting Orode's advances. Described as one of Ogonbiri's most beautiful women, Eloho has dark skin, full lips, and captivating eyes that enhance her glamorous features. Her height is well-proportioned to her weight, and she maintains an elegant style with moderate makeup use. Notably, Eloho is multilingual, fluent in three languages.

Esama's friends and relatives warned her to keep her distance from Eloho. They worried Eloho might try to steal Peregba away, either as a lover or even a second wife. After all, Eloho is beautiful and charming, qualities some saw as a threat to Esama's marriage. Despite their warnings, Esama dismissed them. Unlike the talkative Eloho, Esama is more reserved. Peregba enjoys Eloho's company, but sees her only as his wife's younger sister. Esama trusted both her husband and her friend, believing Eloho would never betray her. However, as Esama and Eloho grew closer, Esama found herself feeling increasingly isolated at home.

I trust my husband completely. He wouldn't even consider touching Eloho," Esama would respond to her friends' concerns. "And Eloho wouldn't even dare look at my husband with romantic interest, especially since she calls him 'Uncle Pere.'" Esama's trust proved justified, as Peregba remained loyal.

Leading the delegation of mothers from Ogonbiri was Matron Etobo. The women brought gifts for Esama and the baby.

"I'm confident his leg will be straightened before he turns three," Matron Etobo declared in her opening remarks. She then turned to Esama. "There have been twenty births in the community these past two weeks, and only two are boys! Boys are like gold here in Ogonbiri. In fact, I already have my gran'daughter picked out as a future wife for your son."

Two other mothers also expressed interest in their daughters marrying Esama's son, Mudiaga. They lamented the predominance of girls being born recently.

Esama, who had been feeling down since giving birth, couldn't help but laugh as the women playfully fought over who their daughters would marry in the future.

'Abeg, leave my innocent son alone,' Esama said with a smile.

Food and drinks were served to the guests. The women brought firewood and various food items like garri, fish, potatoes and tubers of yam and a hunter brought a grasscutter which Esama's mother used in cooking peppersoup for the guests.

'How come women swear in the maternity ward that they will never get pregnant again when they are suffering from labour pains. But, about a week later, they are already enticing their husbands to touch them so that they can get pregnant again?' the matron asked rhetorically. She turned to Esama and said:
"Look at you now, all dolled up with red lipstick and powder..." 'No ooo. I dress fine for my fellow women and my two beautiful children. Not because of my husband," Esama countered.

Don't lie," Peregba joked as he approached his wife and gave her a warm hug. "She dresses up for me!"

Even the black patch on the left part of Esama's face was hidden beneath her elaborate makeup. Peregba then addressed the guests,
"Expect another ceremony like this next year!"
'Nooooo!' Esama exclaimed, bursting into laughter.
'We will start preparing for next year's visit,' mama Etobo stated as she gulped down the second big bottle of Fanta. She continued eating starch and banga soup before finishing off two more bottles of Malt-drink before the ceremony ended.

'Yeeesss oooo!' chorused the women.
'Please, mummy matron, we will need your help for the boy's treatment,' Peregba told the matron who was busy eating starch and banga soup.

If this were an oil-producing community, the oil companies would fly the boy abroad for treatment," the matron remarked.

'Ah! Ah! Ah!' Esama laughed. 'Which oil community? I'm from Enwen oil-producing community. Oil companies do nothing but evil to the community people.' Esama stated. 'I experienced it.

And my husband too. See my burnt face from the burst gas flare. The oil company didn't do anything.'

Esama's spirit was quite uplifted.

'You have not told the women the golden boy's name,' Eloho reminded Esama.

'Oh, I apologize. Matron Etobo and our great women, the baby's name is Mudiaga,' Esama announced.

'What does the name mean because we don't give meaningless names to our children,' Matron Etobo inquired.

'It means "stand firm, stand strong" in our language,' Peregba explained. He added: 'We believe the boy will stand firm on his two legs and he will become a great man in future.'

'Great name. The child will be healed and Mudiaga he shall be.'

'And his *Oyibo* name is Samson.'

'Powerful stand strong Samson!' the women chorused as they stood up to leave. After the closing prayer, guests presented gifts and envelopes containing cash for the newborn baby.

Eloho noticed the sadness on Esama's face after the guests left because of the baby's physical deformity and she told Esama:

'If you don't like the child, dash me na!'

Esama handed Eloho a set of keys. "These are Uncle Orode's house

keys. You'll be staying there with his son, Uvo."

"You're sending me to Uncle Orode's?"

"That's right. You wouldn't want to sleep in our kitchen, would you?" "No, of course not," Eloho responded.

Ogonbiri, a riverine community in Eko Local Government Area, lies within the oil-rich Olobiri State of Abazon, West Africa. Unlike five of the six communities in the local government area, Ogonbiri lacks oil and gas reserves. While some residents, particularly young people like Peregba, lament this absence, others, especially those from nearby oil-producing communities like Esama, view Ogonbiri's lack of resources as a positive. They point to the challenges faced in their own communities, like Eko, the headquarters roughly twenty kilometres away. Ziribiri, the community closest to Ogonbiri, sits along the Ododo-Eko highway, accessible before reaching Ogonbiri. Residents of both communities primarily rely on farming and fishing. Every morning, men and women departed for their farms, separated by a flowing river. Planting seasons in Ogonbiri are cyclical, with farmers sowing cassava, yam, cocoyam, and potatoes between November and December. When the rains arrive around May, flooding becomes a concern from July onwards, prompting harvests before crops rot. Transportation of produce has always been a challenge, where canoes become important and useful. Goods are loaded onto canoes and transported across the river to where pickup trucks or lorries await to take them to Ododo, the state capital.

When crude oil or hydrocarbon and gas were discovered in Eko community about five years ago, the once tranquil rural farming and fishing community dramatically transformed into a hub of industrial activities. The establishment of an oil well and a gas flare cone illuminated the community at night, serving not only as symbols of industrialization, but also as practical resources for activities such as drying fish and processing cassava into *kpokpogarri*. In terms of employment, the community head and his council of elders ensured that all junior staff positions were given to them by the oil company and they subcontracted the jobs to indigenes of other communities. These non-indigenes of Eko community essentially bought the jobs, paying about thirty percent of their monthly salary to Eko community chiefs. These "ghost workers" were employed by Saturn Oil Company.

Peregba, with only two credits in his Abazon Senior School Certificate examination, sought employment in Eko community after realizing he could not afford to retake the exam or pursue tertiary education. He eventually secured a "ghost worker" position as a labourer in the company. With his little earnings, he managed to complete his late father's uncompleted building in Ogonbiri. Unfortunately, upon moving in with his mother, his late father's halfbrothers forced him to leave the compound.

The first rift between the management of Saturn Oil Company and members of Eko community started when there was an oil spillage. The labourers tasked with cleaning up the spill were promised additional compensation, but disputes arose when the promised payments were not made. Indigenes of Enwen community whose farmlands and fish ponds were destroyed by the spillage were promised compensations. However, Mr. Bamdele, the community liaison officer, refused to pay the labourers the extra allowance and the farmers were never compensated. The contractor stated that the council of elders refused to release the money given to them by the contractor. The contractor said he used to buy wheel barrows and shovels. Peregba led a group of the labourers to the contractor to demand for their monies. The contractor's office was located in the premises of the oil company and the security operatives beat up the rioters, injured and detained Peregba. Peregba was dismissed. By then, he was already developing affection for Esama who was staying with her mother.

One of the problems the community had was the delivery of children with physical and mental developmental disorders. Esama made up her mind not to marry male indigenes of Eko community. It was also during this period that one of the gas flare cones was engulfed by fire and Esama sustained burnts. When Peregba encouraged Esama that they should relocate to Ogonbiri, she happily obliged Peregba's request. Esama's family members gave their daughter and Peregba their blessings and they relocated to Ogonbiri. They agreed to raise children after they have stabilized financially. Esama delivered her first child who is a baby girl named Ese. Esama said she has no reason to regret because her first baby, a beautiful girl named Ese, was neither physically nor mentally disabled. Esama recollected that it was about five years after Saturn Oil Company started exploitation of crude oil and gas in Eko community that the delivery of babies with deformities began.

Chapter Three

Peregba and Esama's Efforts to treat their Disabled Son

When Mudiaga was four months old, his mother took him to the health centre in Eko community for vaccination against the primary diseases like measles, chicken pox, small pox and polio. She then decided to remind Matron Etobo about her promise to play invaluable role in ensuring that Mudiaga's bent leg is straightened by a bone doctor. When she arrived *God Saves Maternity Home*, Esama noticed that the medical facility looked deserted. As she entered, Esama saw Priye in her nurse uniform and she sat on matron Etobo's seat.

"Where's Mummy Etobo?" Esama asked Priye after exchanging pleasantries.
"Mummy went for treatment for her diabetes, which has badly affected her left leg, at the Central Hospital in Ododo," Priye responded. "The doctors want to cut off her left leg. She was supposed to be here by now."
"Mummy should watch what she eats," Esama observed.
"She drinks sugary drinks and eats sweet biscuits like groundnut all the time. Did you know she drank two Fanta and two Malt drinks at your baby naming ceremony?"
"What? That was too much! And some people didn't get drinks. My husband bought another crate of minerals."
"Mummy's here!" Priye jumped up from her seat and ran outside.
Matron Etobo walked with a limp like a lady with elephantiasis.
'Welcome mummy,' Esama greeted the matron.

"Priye, no more sugary drinks," Matron Etobo told her assistant. "The doctor is still threatening to cut off my leg if I don't control my diabetes."

"Mummy, we need you around," Esama pleaded.

"My daughter, how have you been coping with the baby?" Matron Etobo asked. She then stood up and went to check on the baby on his mother's back. The matron noticed that Mudiaga's body wasn't properly aligned.

Esama said she was always ashamed when she puts Mudiaga on her back because the twisted leg is always like an excrescence on her back. Anybody that sees the baby on her back definitely knows the baby has some form of deformity since it is only Mudiaga's right leg that was visible on her back. The prominent protrusion of the left leg attracts attention and ridicule of the public. Matron Etobo wondered if Esama wasn't ashamed to carry a disabled child.

"That was before," Esama responded. "I used to carry him on my shoulder, but it got heavier and heavier the farther I walked. I'm not ashamed anymore."

"Yes! Don't care about what people say if you want to live your life," the matron advised Esama.

Esama added that the baby's biggest problem was that when he slept on his back, the weight of his left thigh would press the bent part of the leg, causing him to scream in pain. Just then, Peregba came to the Maternity home.

'How is Obere?' matron Etobo asked Peregba.

'Oh! my late mother-in-law? She died last month,' responded Pergba.

Esama burst into tears when she remembered her mother's death. The next day, Matron Etobo, Peregba, Esama and the baby travelled to Eko in a *Keke*, a three-wheeled motorcycle taxi, to the Saturn Oil Company. From the park, they could see the yellow gas flare and the oil well that are close to each other. There was a *Keke* park and motor park within the same enclosure. The vehicles were mainly for conveying foodstuff from farmlands. However, there were also a few relatively new Toyota Sienna buses that conveyed passengers to the state capital and other adjoining towns. In front of the park were kiosks selling roasted plantains and fish. Women sold bread, kpokpogari (cassava flour snack), and children hawked pure water and minerals. Flies buzzed around the snails and fried pork being hawked. The ground was inundated by dirt and some men were urinating into a nearby shallow gutter overflowing with dirt. The sellers rushed towards the *Keke* Peregba and his family boarded and they were poking bread, chinchin, pure water and fried yam, fried potato and plantain towards them, trying to make sales.

'Buy o. Hot fried yam, fresh bread, cold pure water,' they called out. The women and children selling the items wore dirty clothes and their hair looked unkempt.

'We no want buy, abegiii!' responded Esama angrily.
Matron Etobo carried Mudiaga throughout the trip. When they got to the Eko community relations clinic of Saturn Oil Company, Peregba told the security guard they wanted to see the doctor or nurse in charge. The car park was tarred and flowers were planted by the wall. The wall and the white paint on the two buildings of the clinic looked sparkling clean.

Peregba, a former employee of the Saturn Oil Company, now juggled several jobs to support his family: Keke repair, wheelbarrow repair, bicycle repair, vulcanizing tires, and fishing.

When the security guard, a soldier from Ziribiri, saw Peregba, he made a rude joke about Peregba's multiple occupations. The soldier's aggressive behaviour was calmed down by Esama explaining their urgent need for medical attention for their son.

'Jack of all trade,' laughed the soldier who is from Ziribiri community.
'You be militant or thief,' the soldier asked Peregba.

'People write thief or militant for their face?' Peregba asked the soldier.

'Bloody civilian. I shoot you and you die for nothing,' barked the bulky soldier.

Please, calm down. I want my son to be well, abeg. No quarrel,' Esama pleaded.

Matron Etobo, thankfully, had a connection at the clinic.
'Nurse Tobi is my daughter,' the matron told the soldier.
'Sorry ma, you people should fill the form and come inside,' the security guard told the visitors.

The office was very cold due to the two split unit air conditioners in it, giving it a stark contrast to the harsh conditions they had endured outside. There were eight beds in the room on a row of four on each side. The nurse registered Peregba and charged him two hundred Abazon dollars for the payment of card and consultation with the doctor.

Dr. Musa, the oil company doctor, examined Mudiaga and revealed that he was an orthopedic surgeon, which caused Esama to believe their problems were solved. However, Dr. Musa's role at the oil company had shifted, and he could only offer a referral letter to a distant orthopedic hospital in Ibusa.

'I'm a bone specialist that the medical profession calls an orthopaedic surgeon and...'

'Thank God. Mudiaga's problem is solved,' stated Mudiaga's mother with a grin.

'Sorry, I now write referral letters as an oil company executive,' Dr Musa told the Peregba's family. He promised to give the family a referral letter to the orthopaedic hospital in Ibusa in the Eastern part of the country.

Peregba was outraged. Here they were, from an oil-producing community, and the oil company doctor couldn't even help their child directly. He questioned why the government wasn't using their tax money to build proper medical facilities for the people.

'So, you cannot help a child from the oil producing community that your oil company deformed?' Peregba asked the doctor.

"We pay heavy tax to your government to build medical facilities. Your government should be able to treat your people,"the bone specialist responded

Disappointed, they left the clinic.

When Mudiaga clocked nine months, his leg deformity had worsened. Orode, a friend, suggested to Peregba that the child should be taken to the traditional bone healer. Peregba had earlier approached Matron Etobo to seek help from the traditional ruler to raise funds for them to take Mudiaga to the orthopaedic hospital since they could not raise the sum of about fifty thousand Abazon dollars for the trip to Ibusa and for the treatment. They met the traditional ruler in Eko who also ruled over Ogonbiri and showed Mudiaga's deformed leg to him. However, the ruler offered no assistance, leaving them with few choices. King Oruma burst into hilarious laughter and said:

'Oil company contract money is to make the community better. Many children are born blind, deaf and crippled. Some cannot talk well or read well. Everybody with such problem should take care of their children,' said Oruma.

'Let us take Mudiaga to the traditional bone doctor,' Peregba's best friend concluded.

When the baby was taken to the village where the traditional bone doctor treated patients, Mudiaga's parents were told the old man died about a month ago. However, his son, Akpo, offered to treat Mudiaga despite lacking his father's skills and experience.

'To treat bone is in my blood. I will treat the small boy,' Akpo boasted. Akpo's methods were concerning. He placed Mudiaga on a mat in the mud house with rusted zinc and tied the leg without first straightening it, causing the baby pain and discomfort. Orode was forced to ask Akpo why he didn't straighten the leg first before tying it, Akpo stated that the leg will straighten on its own. Peregba said they should be patient with the treatment for a week. However, Mudiaga was always crying and Esama had difficulty feeding the nine months old baby.

When Matron Etobo came to see baby Mudi and his mother, she was horrified to see how emaciated mother and son had become. Mudiaga was malnourished and had sores from being forced to sleep on his stomach with a makeshift contraption on his leg. Matron Etobo insisted on removing Mudiaga from Akpo's care. It took a month for Mudiaga to recover from the ordeal.

Financial strain took a toll on the family. Esama grew in frustration and vented her anger on her son. She could no longer maintain her smoked fish business due to the time and emotional burden of caring for Mudiaga. As the baby was trying to stand on one leg by holding the chairs in the parlour and trying to walk, Peregba felt that there will be the need to get the boy a small pair of crutches. A carpenter in the community decided to make a light pair of crutches made of plywood for the boy.

Chapter Four

Mudiaga's First Contact with Books

Mudiaga used to follow his father to his workshop when he was five years old. His father repairs bicycles, wheelbarrows and tricycles. Peregba also sells second-hand bicycles and has a vulcanizing machine. However, Mudiaga was always fascinated by the handcraft of the man known as the best craftsman in the entire local government council. The craftsman's workshop was close to Mudiaga's father's workshop. This craftsman, Oyegba inherited the craftsmanship from his father, and he still uses his father's compound by the road to Ona River as his workshop. He moulds flower vase which people come from the city to buy. He moulds and burns cooking pot of various sizes known as *ephere* and *oche*. *Ephere* were small earthen pots used for thickening banga soup or peppersoup before serving it with eba, akpu or starch or yam and unripe plantain. He also makes wicker fish traps of various sizes which are popularly known as *ugen*, sieves for sieving both fried and unfried garri, brooms of various sizes, and mats and baskets woven from rafia materials. The compound was well-organised. There is a shed in the eastern part of the compound where raw materials are stored. On the right side is a shed for finished products like clay pots, flower vase, different sizes and types of wicker fish traps among others. Even at five years old, Mudiaga noticed the steady flow of people that come to supply raw materials like palm tree and raffia tree fonds for making brooms and materials for making the other products. Mudiaga, who used to walk with the aid of crutches made of plyboard, is always fascinated by the number of customers that buy Oyegba's products in large quantities, especially on market days.

Mudiaga would often tug on his father's shirt, stopping him so that he could admire Oyegba's crafts. Oyegba, noticing the young boy's interest, said to Peregba, 'Let the boy come and stay with me and look at how I work.'
'Okay.' He looked at Mudiaga and asked:
'You will come here?'
'Yes,' answered Mudiaga with a broad smile on his face.
The next day, Mudiaga's father dropped Mudiaga at the crafts workshop and told his son.
'Hungry? Come and eat at my workshop.'

Mudiaga nodded his head in the affirmative. Mudiaga had become closer to his father and Ese, his elder sister. He perceived that his mother hates him and the relationship between mother and son had become frosty. Mudiaga now enthusiastically looks forward to going to Oyegba's crafts shop. Oyegba, a man in his forties, is short, fat and barded. He has two wives and seven children. He is however not a happy man because none of his four sons is interested in pursuing their father's profession.
******

Mudiaga's first contact with books was from his elder sister's old picture books. One of them is titled: *A – Z in Pictures* where A is for apple. He wondered what a real apple looks like although he had seen the picture of an apple in the book. He was also fascinated by his elder sister's two colour books. He instantly became fascinated with pictures and paintings. One day, he was not feeling well; so, he decided to stay at home alone. He grabbed one of his sister's books and went outside, intending to scribble on the sand with a pencil. Mudiaga flipped happily through the pages, occasionally copying pictures from the book onto the ground. The weather was a bit cloudy but he presumed the rain will not fall yet. In an instant, the heavens opened up and it started raining heavily. Before Mudiaga could stand up with the aid of his crutches and tried to pick the drawing book, it has already been soaked by the rain. He struggled to go into the house and laid the book open on the floor in the living room, hoping that it would dry before his sister returned from school. However, some of the paintings were already blurred beyond repair by the rain.

Mudiaga looking at Ese's picture book outside the house

When Ese came from school and noticed that her drawing book was wet, she was angry with her brother, but their close relationship prevented her from getting physical with him. It was a different story when Mudiaga's mother and father came home. Esama saw the book and she was livid with anger:
'What do you think you can do in life with drawing on the floor? You will be beggar or shoe maker.Bad luck boy for life! '

Mudiaga burst into tears and wondered why he was unlucky to be born with a disability. His sister consoled him and his father, much calmer, promised to buy him new picture books. This news made Mudiaga ecstatic.

Mudi's father reassured his son that education is important. He promised Mudiaga he will go to school first to learn how to read and write and will learn crafts in *Oyegba's Craft Shop* whenever he is free as he grows older. True to his words, Peregba bought two new picture books for Mudiaga, who was very excited. Mudiaga kept the books carefully inside a nylon bag to avoid getting them wet again. 'Draw, draw,' Ese playfully called Mudiage his pet name.

'Me draw big far far,' declared Mudiaga, pointing his finger forward.
'Yes. Future big painter and craftsman,' Peregba stated proudly.
'Papa. Mama. I draw you. I draw mama.'
'Abeg, abeg, no draw me oo! I don't want to look like juju or spirit oo!' Esama told his son. She showed Mudiaga a physically fit son she delivered about a year ago. 'See my first son. Not you.'
'Draw me my son,' responded Pergba. 'Even if I look like juju, I will be proud that my son drew me.'
So, no drawing of me?' Ese asked with a frown while pointing at Mudiaga.
'I draw Ese.' Mudiaga replied sweetly, causing Ese to smile broadly.

Chapter Five

Mudiaga Goes to School

A day before Mudiaga was to go to school when he was six years old, Peregba called Esama for a discussion about ensuring his son's smooth first day at school. Peregba knew that Mudiaga could not walk the one thousand metres distance to school with crutches. Determined to encourage his son's education, Peregba decided to carry Mudiaga to and from school each day.

'You want to carry this cripple to school and bring him back every day?' Esama enquired.

Her resentment towards Mudiaga had become more evident since the birth of their able-bodied son.

'Whether he is a cripple or not, he has shown interest in learning and I will not deprive him of the opportunity,' Mudiaga's father asserted.
'By the way, who told you he is a cripple? He can walk.' Esama's response was laced with bitterness.

'Now, I have a whole son. A son without any comma and not half man like Mudiaga,' Esama stated.

'I will run away. I've not decided whether I will not run away. Just that the priestess of Olokun told me that Mudi will one day walk like a normal human being.'

The next morning, Peregba carried Mudi on his shoulder, holding Mudiaga's plywood crutches in one hand. Ese who was in Primary three followed behind. When they arrived at the school, Peregba put his son down and Mudiaga walked into the school with the aid of his crutches. Part of the fence of the Primary school had fallen and the school compound was overgrown with weeds. Peregba met the headmistress who directed them to Primary one. Peregba noticed that many children riveted their gaze at Mudiaga. The headmistress directed the Primary Five and Six pupils to go into the classrooms to kill the lizards and other creatures in the classrooms since most of the doors of the six classrooms lack locks. In addition, most of the wooden windows have fallen off. The roofs of the classrooms were on the brink of collapse and leaky zinc panels resulted in pools of water in two classrooms.

Chaos erupted in a nearby Primary Four classroom. Pupils yelled 'Snake! Snake! Snake!' and ran outside, two even jumping out of the window. A male teacher led some boys to the class and they killed the medium-sized green snake. The boys killed lizards, rats and the girls then swept the classrooms. The pupils were warned not to play in the overgrown field.

Primary 1 classroom presented a bleak picture. The peeling yellow paint hung off the walls and most of the desks were broken. Logs of wood were used to support the broken legs of the benches. On the last roll in front are logs used to improvise the shortage of seats. The blackboard relied on a simple rag used as a duster. Mr. Zikiye, the Primary 1 teacher, wondered why there are not enough seats despite the fact that parents pay for seats. The windows are wooden and there are two sets on each side, with a broken hinge on one. A makeshift support, a simple stick, held it barely shut. The oncefenced school compound was now a mess. Half the fence had collapsed, leaving a gaping hole that allowed easy access for animals. Chickens and goats frequently wandered into the school compound. The two-block school building itself wasn't much better. Large cracks marred one block, and Mudiaga noticed holes in the roof that would surely leak whenever rain falls. From the road to the school compound there is a wooden bridge but it is not used by the students since this is dry season. It means that during the rainy season pupils and teachers will have to walk gingerly on the wooden bridge since the ground will be inundated by water.

The headmistress is a fat black and short woman in her middle age. She is simply known as headmistress by teachers, pupils and parents, and comes to school only three times a week from the state capital. Boldly written on her table is "Mrs. Diobu, Headmistress". Mrs. Diobu was pessimistic about Mudiaga staying in school for more than a month since most disabled children stop school after a short while because they cannot withstand ridicule and bullying. Peregba, however, remained confident and assured her that Mudiaga loved learning and wouldn't give up on school.

'My son like book well well. He will not stop school,' Peregba assured the headmistress.

'Let us wait and see,' remarked Mrs Diobo, the headmistress, as she gave Peregba the list of books and the cost of desk and uniform.
Mudiaga's teacher, Mr. Zikiye was a young man of about twenty, fresh out of secondary school. He just wants to teach for about a year or two before he leaves for the University for his degree programme. He also wants to rewrite his Senior Secondary School examination since he did not make credit in Mathematics and Economics. Mr Zikiye has been having a running battle with his father. While Zikiye wanted to study Fine and Applied Arts, his father insisted that he must study a different course or else he would not pay Zikiye's school fees if he insisted on learning 'drawing', as his father described Fine and Applied Arts. . Zikiye then decided to study Political Science. Zikiye has a personal connection with disability. Thus, he has a soft spot for disabled people because his mother was involved in an accident about five

years ago and she has remained bound to a wheelchair. A rapport instantly developed between Mudiaga and Mr. Zikiye. Except for three repeaters, the pupils in Primary 1 had not yet donned their uniforms. The leader of this group of repeaters was Uvo, a ten year old repeating Primary 1 for the third time. He sat on the front row and nobody wanted to share a seat with him, but since the fifteen double desks and benches were not enough for the about forty pupils, a girl had to share Mudiaga's desk with him. The girl's name is Batowei. Some of the pupils sat on cut timber while others sat on broken benches.

The very first day, Mudiaga faced the harsh reality of bullying. Uvo bullied Mudiaga thus:

'I troway. Your firewood leg. 'One leg. Half leg.' Uvo mocked Mudiaga. Uvo was sitting directly behind Mudiaga. He is the tallest and oldest in his class. He is thickset in physique, black in complexion and is square-faced.

'Half brain. You are repeating Primary one for the third time and cannot speak well,' Zikiye pointed pugnaciously at Uvo. He added that: 'It is better to be physically disabled than to be mentally disabled.'

'Sir. Me. Well well well,' and he touched his body while laughing. 'You are not well at all at all,' Zikiye taunted Uvo. He added: 'Ten years and a third year in Primary one.'

The teacher turned to Mudi and told him that he must try and spend the session in school so that he can stand out among the disabled children that completed Primary one as far as the record of the enrolment of disabled children is concerned. Zikiye said other disabled pupils spend either at most one term or less than a term. Mudiaga nodded his head in the affirmative.

Before closing time, Peregba arrived to carry his son home. He had cobbled together a makeshift tricycle to take Mudiaga's to school, but he knew the plan wouldn't work during the rainy season. He decided that Mudiaga will not be going to school regularly once the rain starts falling.

By the third week, Mudi's father had bought him a few books. Mudiaga was really fascinated by the picture and drawing books. Then, in the fourth week, Mudi told Mr Zikiye that he wouldn't be returning to school because his father struggled to carry him back and forth every day.

'Did your father complain?' Mr Zikiye asked.

'No.'

'Continue your education. I see you looking at your picture books all the time and you try to draw.

You want to succeed, don't listen to people. I will buy another colour book and colour pencil for you,' Zikiye assured Mudi.

On the morning Mudi was supposed to stop school, Zikiye appeared in front of Peregba's home to roll Mudi to school. Within two weeks, many students come to Pere's home to follow Zikiye and the senior pupils who derive joy in rolling Mudi to school.

'You're now a celebrity,' Zikiye told Mudi.

'Ehn, ehn?' wondered Mudi.

'I mean you're now popular.'

'Thank you sir. You give me heart. Not to stop school,' Mudiaga
told Zikiye.

An unlikely friendship blossomed between Uvo and Mudiaga. Uvo
noticed that Mudi was always fascinated and excited any time he
saw the picture of a boy catching fish in his book.

'You like. Catch fish?' Uvo asked Mudi.
'Yes. Yes ooo!' responded Mudi.
'Satodi. I come. We go. Catch fish,' stated Uvo.
'Come o. Come o' pleaded Mudi.

On a Saturday morning, as promised by Uvo, he and his elder
cousin came to visit and they told Mudi's father that they want to
go on a fishing expedition with him. Uvo became Mudiaga's best
friend because Mudiaga patiently picks Uvo's splintered
utterances which are always sentence fragments. Mudiaga fills
the gaps and understands Uvo. It turned out that Uvo's father and
Peregba were once neighbours when Mudiaga was born. Uvo's
mother, fearing she might have another disabled child, left her
husband when Uvo was about two years old. Although Uvo
occasionally visited his father, he never knew Mudiaga would
attend the same school. Uvo's family had built a house at the far
end of Ogonbiri, by the bank of the Ona River.

Despite Peregba's apprehension, Mudiaga was adamant about
being safe. As a compromise, Peregba insisted Ese accompany
them in case of any mishaps. Ese reassured her father that
Mudiaga would be alright. Uvo and his cousin showed Mudiaga
the fishing hook and a can of earthworms they'd be using as bait.
They explained that when the float submerged, it meant a fish
was caught, and Mudiaga would need to reel in the line.

This wasn't Mudiaga's first fishing experience. At four years old, he'd accompanied his family to the Kpakiama fishing community. His father explained the two fishing seasons: May to July and October to early December. The first coincided with the rainy season's arrival, while the second marked the dry season's beginning. Strict rules governed the oil communities. The most sacred was the prohibition of using herbicides to catch fish. This practice killed all aquatic life, including small fish, and contaminated the remaining fish, making them unfit for consumption.

Mudiaga was fascinated by the big trees and the communal lifestyle in the oil fishing community. Peregba and Esama rented a small room where the entire family stayed for two weeks before they returned to Ogonbiri. On the day the couple went fishing, they brought the children to stay under the shade of a big tree near the fishing site. In the evening, the couple sent their catch for drying and they kept the fish that had been dried. Two weeks after they returned from the fishing expedition, Esama carried the smoked fish to Ododo city to sell with a higher profit margin. Mudiaga noticed that the children he met there did not discriminate against him and he really enjoyed his stay in the fishing community. There were four moonlight nights and the children gathered to play under the moonlight. Adolescents had their different play sessions and circles. He vividly recalled one morning when his mother forgot fresh fish for the planned pepper soup breakfast. She rushed to the stream with her wicker fish basket and returned in thirty minutes with six medium-sized fish.

Another time, Peregba carried Mudiaga on his shoulder to observe the fishing techniques. He saw people not only dip long sticks into holes near the roots of large trees but also work in muddy ponds. Women waded through the mud, pulling their baskets through the water. Upon raising the baskets, they'd have fish inside. Each woman would empty her catch into a marked container, then return to the river or pond to continue. Large mudfish would surface for air, and young men with cutlasses would be ready to catch them.

Additionally, a group of women specialized in drying the fish.

During these two seasons, people relocate to the fishing communities where there are many rivers that discharge their waters into a pool from where the water then flows to the Atlantic Ocean. The first feature of Kpakiama seasonal fishing community is the fact that there are many swamp dwelling trees and it is under these trees that the fishes stay.

After Mudiaga followed Uvo and his cousin to fish on two occasions, Uvo came alone one day and he said the two of them should go fishing. His father was not at home and Ese was not interested in following them. Uvo held one of Mudiaga's hands while Mudiaga held the one clutch on his bad leg. Uvo carried a backpack where he kept his cup of worms. He had two slim raffia sticks with the rope of the hook and its floater showing in the middle. When they went fishing the last time, they found a perfect spot that Mudiaga can sit and do his fishing conveniently without any fear of him falling into the river because there was a stump of wood he sat on while in his front there is a fallen tree that was higher than the stump of wood he was sitting on the stump of wood. The stomp of wood and the higher wood in front of Mudiaga were like Mudiaga's bench and desk in class. Mudiaga can vividly see the river directly in front of him. Where he sat, it seems the water has diverted to the spot because about two metres in front of him, he noticed a large expanse of water flowing downstream. Luckily enough for Mudi, there was a tree whose shade covered him and Uvo. Mudiaga inserted a half worm in the hook. He threw the hook in the river. He waited for a minute. Then he noticed the floater dipping into the river and popping out. The floaters deepened under the water. Mudiaga drew his hook and caught a medium sized catfish.

Mudiaga at a fishing spot with Uvo. He drew out a fish with Uvo shouting

'Draw' 'Draw!' screamed Uvo.

Mudiaga drew the hook. He saw a medium sized catfish wriggling. He found it difficult to remove the hook from the mouth of the fish. Uvo did not help him. Uvo was just laughing as Mudiaga eventually removed the fish from the hook after the fish had stung him twice. Blood gushed out from one of Mudiaga's fingers.

'Lick. The blood,' Uvo instructed Mudiaga.

''Phw, plw plw,' Mudiaga spat out the blood he sucked into his mouth.

'Oh, your blood. Bitter?' Uvo asked Mudiaga. 'My Blood. My. Sweet,' Uvo laughed.

'Are you a mosquito or blood-sucking animal?' Mudiaga asked his friend. 'I will soon start running away from you. You can kill me. And suck my blood.'

'I, lion?' Uvo asked Mudiaga. 'Hook. Always shook. Your hand. Fish bone. Shook you. From the mouth of the fish.' 'So, I will see my blood every day,' Mudiaga observed.

'Yes ooo!' laughed Uvo.

The next fish Mudiaga caught was a big mud fish. They stayed at the fishing spot for about four hours before they decided to go home. As they emerged from the foot path that led them to the river and got to the wider foot path, a woman told them to sell their catch to her.

'Sell. Small,' Uvo advised Mudiaga.

When Mudiaga got home with the fish and the money, he gave them to his father. His father, however, returned the money and asked him to keep it.

'My son caught all this fish?' Esama asked her son with a smile when she saw the fish Mudiaga caught.

Mudiaga was bewildered when he noticed his mother's change of countenance towards him.

"Let me keep your money for you,' Esama told her son.

'Don't chop the boy's money,' Peregba told his wife.

'My son's money is my money,' Esama stated emphatically.
Mudiaga was quite amused by the fact that his fishing expedition has now elicited lively discussions in the home. He made up his mind to buy more drawing books and raffia that he would use to produce seavers and wickerfish traps. He now hopes to focus on his fishing, drawing and weaving.

That evening, Mudiaga was given delicious banga soup with a big fresh dish and eba to eat. This was the first his mother really pampered him.

'Anytime you catch big fish like this, you will eat half of the fish,' Mudiaga's mother told her son.

Mudiaga was surprised to note that the small earthen pot that he made with Oyegba's assistance as part of his apprenticeship was the one that his mother served his banga soup in. Esama had condemned the pot and kept it away. Ese's soup was served in a plate and the size of her fish was much smaller than that of Mudiaga. She poured her soup into Mudiaga's earthen pot and she started eating with her younger brother.

'You're my dream sister. You've really made me happy. You followed me to my first fishing lesson.'

Meanwhile, Ese swapped the fish in the earthen pot. She told Mudiaga to eat the small fish.

'I will not complain my sister,' responded Mudiaga and they continued eating in silence.

Mudiaga knows that he has uncle Zikiye and Uvo to thank for making him develop his self-confidence. He noticed that he has now discovered the things that he can do enthusiastically. They are fishing, drawing and creating art works.

At night, Mudiaga had a dream and found himself at the spot where he used to catch fish. He rediscovered himself trying to remove the catfish that stung him from the hook. As he removed the catfish from the hook, the cat fish stung Mudiaga again. Its size increased astronomically. The catfish gave Mudiaga a bear hug. The fish pulled him into the river. With the fish in front, Mudiaga was led to the bottom of the river. They swam to the bottom of a tree. Mudiaga saw some fishes that are siblings and parents of the catfish he caught the previous day. The catfish introduced Mudiaga to other fishes. They swam under the big tree and it was there that Mudiaga joined in a meeting with the other fishes and the head of the fishes noted that they would soon be displaced from their present habitat and it urged them that they should all swim downstream to a spot that will not be affected by the event. But one of the fishes complained that the further they travel downstream, the closer they will be to the Ocean. The salty water close to the Ocean would not be good for their existence. The fishes concluded that they would join another river as they swam downstream.

Mudiaga noticed a giant machine uprooted the tree they were staying under. Mudiaga and all the fishes fell close to one another. Mudiaga and the fish he caught the previous day were looking for the spot Mudiaga sat when he caught the catfish and they eventually found the spot. Mudiaga got to where he believed his home was and he was shocked to discover that machines had pulled down the houses. Mudiaga woke up. He was sweating profusely. Mudiaga was so scared. He informed his father about the dream. Peregba went to consult matron Etobo who was also a seer in the community. 'The spirit of the fish is already in your son's body,' the matron told Mudiaga's father.

'Only Oil Company can destroy the Ogonbiri community and nobody will resist because the oil company is protected by soldiers,' Peregba observed.

Mudiaga told his father that some men that wore white helmets and orange overalls had come to measure the school land on two occasions. Mudiaga added that on one occasion, they were told to stay indoors while the sound of a big gun reverberated. Peregba told his son that the people that he saw were workers of a Seismic company searching for oil and gas deposits.

'There is no crude oil in Ogonbiri,' Peregba assured his son. He added: 'Nobody will bring machines to destroy our home. That fish is a spirit fish but we don't see any sign that the flow of water will be diverted from our community.'

The first time Mudiaga went fishing alone, his father was worried but the place is always busy and the young boys that usually go fishing during the weekends have reserved Mudiaga's space for him; so, whenever he goes fishing, his space is always waiting for him.

Mudiaga usually goes to the stem of a big Mahogany tree whose root is the source of river Agamen. There are some men who are worshippers of the tree. There are many fishes in the river but nobody is allowed to kill them. He just sits under the shade and admires the fishes as they swim in and out of the root of the tree. Further down the stream is a spot where indigenes of Ogonbiri fetch drinking water. Children and women also come to wash plates and clothes. The big Mahogany tree has been named the tree of life. It is believed that the water by the root of the tree has healing powers. Sick individuals meet the priestess of the tree which houses a deity known as Igbunu deity. She fetches water, makes some incantation on the water and the individuals take their bath and drink the water on the spot. They then take some quantity of water home to drink. Some big trees around this particular tree are never touched. Ogonbiri indigenes believe that the sustenance of the community physically and spiritually hinges on the protective powers of the deity in the tree. To Mudiaga, the tree is a refuge and a groove where he can think clearly and let go whatever worries he has. On three occasions, he had attempted to draw the tree and on each occasion the drawing was quite different. Then he noticed that his mood reflects on his drawing of the tree. He is usually awed by the pristine water and peaceful surroundings with birds chirping, monkeys and squirrels jumping from one branch of the tree to another. Legend has it that the sustenance of the community is premised on the tree. The priestess of the tree asserts that the day the tree dies, peace, prosperity and progress will elude the community. The priestess told Mudiaga:

'Nothing will happen to this tree in the next one thousand years.'
****

Mudiaga was overwhelmed with joy when he noticed that he was already in Primary three and he has become a consummate crafts boy and adroit at catching fish with hook. Due to Oyegba's tutelage, Mudiaga had started honing his skills in making small and big earthen pots. Uvo already knew the spot where clay for the pots can be sourced. He brings large quantities of clay and firewood that would be used in drying the clay pots. Mudiaga and Uvo now make fishing hooks with hooks of different sizes and ropes and fishing rods of different sizes. The three sizes are small, medium and big sized hooks. The small sized hooks are bought by children between the ages of five and ten years while teenagers and adults can buy the medium and big sized hooks. The size and depth of the water where the individual wants to hook also determines the size of hook to be bought by an individual interested in hooking. Uvo and Mudiaga also make brooms and wicker fish traps, and sieve for sieving unfried and fried garri. They employed women who produce small sized brooms for sweeping homes and big sized brooms for sweeping the outside of compounds. While the small sized brooms are made from fronds of palm trees, the big sized brooms are made from raffia palms. They seek advice from Oyegba who can be described as Mudiaga and Uvo's mentor and consultant.

However, going to school during the rainy season was always a difficult period for Mudiaga. Due to the fact that the ground was soggy, it was quite difficult to push the tricycle even by the senior pupils. So, he was skipping school but he found joy in his painting and the drawing book. However, whenever the weather was bright, he went to school.

Mudiaga has also emerged as Oyegba's most consistent apprentice. This wasn't his only accomplishment. In the classroom, despite his disability, Mudiaga thrived. His strengths perfectly complemented those of his friend, Uvo, who by then was in Primary 2. Together, they formed a formidable team.

Chapter Six

Seismic officials and Soldiers Invade Ogonbiri community

Esama was five months pregnant with her fourth child when she noticed the frenetic activities in Ogonbiri community primary school where she sells food stuff. The lady that used to sell food in the Primary school had relocated to the city. Mudiaga pleaded with his class teacher to inform the headmaster that his mother would love to sell in the school. Mudiaga was loved by the teachers of the school because he was the first disabled pupil that had stayed in the school for more than one year. What was more? Mudiaga and Uvo had always won the arts and craft exhibition that the school organizes at the end of every session. Mudiaga and his friend supplied the school with free long and short brooms. The headmistress invited Mudiaga's mother and told her: 'I love the way you and your husband encourage and support your son.' She added: 'Many women including my sister have applied for this opportunity but I will give you so that you can support Mudiaga more.'

Esama started her food vendor business eight months ago. It had been profitable, so she went to thank Matron Etobo, who had previously advised Esama to love her son. Matron Etobo then offered a proverb: 'This rejected stone might become your chief cornerstone.'

Esama's food stall was located behind the first building of classrooms, with Mudiaga's class (Primary Three) being the last one in that block. She primarily sold rice and beans with two stew options: regular stew with less pepper and a spicy pepper stew. The smaller cooler containing the spicy stew was kept close by, as it was mainly favored by the teachers. The meat pieces were small, earning them the nickname "panadol" (a brand of pain reliever). Each piece cost two Abazon cents. A bucket of water was provided for the students who couldn't afford the three-cent "pure water" (sachets of water). Esama also sold kpokpogarri (cassava snack) and peanuts. Female students often purchased food for the teachers.

While students were on break, some girls were buying food for the teachers when gun-wielding soldiers and men in red overalls suddenly swarmed the school compound. Other students waiting to buy food formed a queue. Sergeant Kokovo, an indigene of Ziribiri (a neighboring community with an ongoing boundary dispute with Esama's community), fired a shot into the air. Students and teachers were confused about the soldiers' presence. Although there had been lingering tension between the two communities, no deaths had resulted from the disputes.The gunshot from Sergeant Kokovo caused a stampede as students scrambled for cover.

The children waiting in line for food panicked and rushed towards Esama's rickety table, knocking it over in the process. All the food spilled onto the ground. The worst part was that the small container of spicy pepper stew splashed onto Esama's face. Pregnant Esama screamed in pain, fearing she'd been blinded.

"My eyes! I can't see! Help me!" she cried out.

Some of the Primary Two pupils also got pepper stew in their eyes and started crying hysterically. Other children were desperately searching the ground for the "panadol"-like meat, while others ate the spilled rice and beans. The loud screams from Esama and the affected pupils continued. Mudiaga, using his crutches, rushed to his mother's side, worried she'd been shot. The excruciating burning sensation from the pepper in Esama's eyes was unbearable.

"Mommy! Mommy!" Mudiaga cried as he attempted to use water to soothe the burning sensation in his mother's eyes. However, his efforts were hampered by needing to hold onto his crutches for balance. Second Lieutenant Musa Dogo found Mudiaga's attempts to help his mother amusing.

Uvo confronted the soldiers' commander, but Sergeant Kokovo pushed him to the ground. The commander then proceeded to the headmistress's office. The headmistress insisted that Esama and Mudiaga be allowed to leave the school grounds so Esama could receive medical attention. She emphasized that Mudiaga was the only disabled student who had remained at her school for more than a year.

Second Lieutenant Musa Dogo scolded the headmistress for not notifying students about the school closure. Seismic workers, searching for potential hydrocarbon deposits, were scheduled to survey the school grounds and discharge test shots that week. Two civilian officials were present: Comrade Bamdele, the community liaison officer for Saturn Oil Company, and Owibo, representing the community council of elders.

"Our nation's livelihood depends on crude oil production," Comrade Bamdele chided the headmistress. "We were surprised to hear you refused to close the school."

"No one informed me the school would be closed this week," the headmistress defended herself.

"Anyone sabotaging this oil search will face a 20-year jail sentence!" Sergeant Kokovo barked.

"Order!" Second Lieutenant Dogo commanded, glancing towards Sergeant Kokovo, who was old enough to be his father.

Panicked parents rushed to the school to collect their children.

Unfortunately, soldiers guarded the broken gate and fence, preventing anyone from entering.

"My wife, the rice seller! My son with the crutch! Ese, my daughter!" Peregba yelled as he barged into the schoolyard. He raced towards his wife, who was crying hysterically from the pepper burns in her eyes.

"If you don't let me take my pregnant wife for treatment, you'll shoot me before you find any oil here! Let her go!" Peregba demanded, his voice firm. He wore blue overalls and safety boots, hinting at his profession.

Recognizing Peregba's seriousness, the soldiers allowed them to leave. Second Lieutenant Dogo ordered Sergeant Kokovo, "Let them go.”

Uvo and Peregba carried Esama out of the schoolyard. Ese followed closely, sobbing uncontrollably at her mother's distress. Peregba feared another miscarriage and rushed his wife to *God Saves Maternity and Nursing Home.*

Matron Etobo sat motionless in a corner of the ward. Amputated five years ago, her left leg remained a constant reminder. Her vision had deteriorated significantly, leaving her nearly blind. Despite her condition, she refused to retire. With Priye gone, Matron Etobo employed a retired nurse. Upon learning about Esama's predicament, Matron Etobo instructed, "Bring two bowls of clean water. Mama Mudi, sit in front of a bowl and splash your face until you can barely breathe.”

Esama rinsed her eyes with clean water for about two hours, the water being changed periodically. Finally, she opened her eyes, regaining her composure. A broad smile spread across her face as she saw her family gathered around her. Esama then remembered that she had bought the ingredients for the food on credit.

"Honey, I bought the rice, beans, and tomatoes I used for the food on credit," she confessed.

"Life first, Mama, Mudi," Uvo declared. He then turned to Mudiaga and said, "We catch. Fish. One. Week. Your mama. Pay . Rice money. Bean money."

"Yes, if we go fishing three times, I'll be able to cover the cost of the wasted food," Mudiaga assured his mother.

"Give me my drink," Matron Etobo instructed her caretaker.

The woman brought a bottle of Fanta with a dark substance mixed in. Matron Etobo took the bottle and drank some.

"Sweetened bitter leaf water!" Matron Etobo declared, smacking her lips.

"Bitter leaf water?" Esama questioned.
"Yes! I avoid sugary drinks now and prefer bitter ones."
Esama groaned, expressing her worry that the Oil Company might soon come to Ogonbiri.

"Those witches," Ese's mother muttered under her breath.
"They're still exploring for oil," Peregba clarified for his wife.
"Mudi, the once rejected son of Peregba's household, is now the cornerstone," Matron Etobo remarked when she learned how the

soldiers allowed the family to leave the school because of Mudiaga's intervention.

"You're absolutely right," Mudi's mother agreed.

All students and staff of Ogonbiri Community Primary School were instructed to stay home for the next three days while the Seismic Company explored for potential crude oil deposits. Teachers and students were held at school until 4:00 PM. The headmistress later learned that the Oil Company had given Comrade Bamdele one hundred thousand Abazon dollars to inform the Ogonbiri community about the Seismic Company's impending operation. However, Comrade Bamdele, Owibo, and community leaders embezzled the money. Neither the community nor the school principal were notified.

Second Lieutenant Dogo, appalled by Esama's ordeal and financial loss, gave the headmaster five thousand Abazon dollars to compensate the owner of the spilled food. Esama was overwhelmed with joy when she received the cash gift a week later.

Chapter Seven

Discovery of Fraudulent Practice by Mudiaga

Six months after Seismic officials and soldiers invaded Ogonbiri community, information filtered throughout Ogonbiri town that reserves of oil and gas had been discovered in the community. Esama, scarred from her near-death experience with a gas flare in Eko, another oil-producing community, worried about having to move again. The scar on her left cheek served as a constant reminder of that harrowing experience. She proposed relocating to a community untouched by oil exploration.

'I will not run away from my community,' Peregba countered. 'I want the oil company to take my son abroad and treat his left leg. I also want to chop oil money.'

'You can dream,' Esama scoffed. She had just delivered a baby girl in good physical condition. She now had four children: two boys and two girls.

The oil company, Saturn Oil, designated a new area for the relocated Ogonbiri community. However, this land encroached upon Ziribiri territory. The Ziribiri elders objected to this forced relocation, claiming it would sow discord between the two communities. They warned that Ogonbiri residents would be treated as outsiders and stripped of their rights. As compensation, Saturn oil Company decided to build a mini housing estate, a new Primary and a model secondary school in the newly built community. Additionally, the company offered scholarships to the top three students in the new primary school to attend the model secondary school. Saturn Oil also planned to build an oil well, a gas flare cone, and a flow station in the section of Ogonbiri slated for demolition.

Within a year, the company aimed to complete the new housing estate, the model primary and secondary school. The estate was named "New Ogonbiri Community". However, the houses would be partially built, with each family receiving funds to finish construction.

Comrade Bamdele, accompanied by Lt. Musa Dogo, held a town hall meeting with representatives from various community wards. As a ward leader, Peregba attended with his son, Mudiaga (now ten years old), and Mudiaga's friend, Uvo (now fifteen years old). Comrade Bamdele announced that the demolition of Old Ogonbiri would begin in a month. He urged families to move into their designated apartments. The ward leaders pleaded for a two-month extension to allow Ogonbiri farmers to harvest and sell their crops before relocating. This would give the community time to prepare psychologically for the move. Comrade Bamdele agreed to take this request to the company's managing director.

The oil company, Saturn Oil, devised a compensation plan. Ogonbiri households whose houses would be demolished or whose farmland would be crossed by pipelines were promised compensation. Owibo, secretary of the Ogonbiri council of elders, collabourated with Comrade Bamdele, an official from the Ministry of Lands and Survey, and another from the Federal Ministry of Petroleum Resources, to create an inventory of households eligible for relocation and compensation. Saturn Oil planned to construct houses on the newly acquired plots of land.

Comrade Bamdele attempted to manipulate the system for personal gain. He convinced Owibo that they could pocket extra money if Owibo persuaded the council of elders to offer a lower cash amount to the families. The plan was for the families to receive a smaller sum upfront and then be responsible for completing the partially built houses themselves, including plastering, installing ceilings, doors, and windows. Finally, the houses would be painted uniformly.

All affected families were instructed to assemble at the primary school premises. Officials sat at a table with chairs facing the families. Each family was given documents to fill out and a form to sign or thumbprint. Peregba attended with Mudiaga. Many family heads were accompanied by their educated children. Uvo, holding his father's hand, was also present. Mudiaga noticed a discrepancy. The cover sheet displayed a compensation amount of one million Abazon dollars, while the document presented for thumbprinting offered only one hundred thousand Abazon dollars. When Peregba received a document stating a total compensation of three hundred thousand dollars, Mudiaga intervened.

'Daddy, don't put your ink hand on the paper,' Mudiaga informed his father. 'The money in the two papers is different.'

'What is wrong with this illiterate cripple?' Comrade Bamdele asked Owibo.

'I don't know for him,' responded Owibo. He told Peregba. 'Don't mind your frustrated cripple son. Put your thumb and collect your free money,'

People in the queue behind Peregba grew impatient, urging him to sign, collect his papers, and move on.

'Sign and commot na,' they chanted.

'Wait small,' Peregba pleaded.

'My father will take the first paper,' Mudiaga insisted. 'That is his money.'

The situation escalated as Sergeant Kokovo, an officer seemingly working with the corrupt officials, approached Peregba angrily.

'Sign the paper. Take your paper and commot the line,'

'Tell oga Owibo to give my father the first paper,' Mudiaga, who was leaning on his crutches, told Sergeant Kokovo.

The remaining families waiting for their compensation became restless, and the atmosphere threatened to erupt into chaos.

'Just wait and let us consult,' Owibo told the crowd.

Owibo, Comrade Bamdele and Lt. Dogo had a brief meeting in one of the classrooms. Sergeant Kokovo and other soldiers guarded the table and the documents on it.

'Why did you allow that one and a half-legged boy see the differences in the two papers his father was to sign?' Owibo queried comrade Bamdele.

'The boy opened the other document and saw the difference. Is the deformed boy Argus?' comrade Bamdele asked.

'Argus? Who is Argus?' Owibo and Lt. Dogo asked in unison.

'Don't mind me. He is a powerful monster in Greek mythology that has eyes all over his body. He can see far. The other boy called Uvo is idiotic, imbecilic, giant gullible gorilla-like fatuous, foolish son named Ares. Ares is the Greek God of war,' noted comrade Bamdele. 'Your abuses can kill the two fools. So, what do we do?'

Lt Dogo asked. 'I can tell Sergeant Kokovo to fire some shots in the air and everybody will run away.'

'No oo,' responded comrade Bamdele. 'Give Mudiaga's father the one million dollars paper. Tell father and son to shut up.' 'Okay,' responded Owibo.
When Peregba was given the one million Abazon dollar document, Mudiaga instructed him to turn to the waiting crowd and yell, "One million dollars!" while holding the paper aloft.
Next person to collect his paper was Uvo's father. Mudiaga had instructed his friend to say
'Give my father paper with one million dollars written on it.'
As Uvo's father was about to thumbprint the papers, Uvo shouted:
'Give. Papa. One. Million. Na. Na,'
Uvo glanced a disdainful look at Sergeant Kokovo who sat behind Owibo. He was meant to protect everybody on the table.
'Give the imbecile boy's father the one million Abazon dollars voucher,' comrade Bamdele instructed Owibo. Uvo took the voucher, raised the voucher up and shouted:
'Million! One! Million!'

This set off a chain reaction. Everyone in line at the school began chanting, "One million dollars! Not one hundred thousand dollars!"

Mudiaga insisting that his father should be given one million Abazon dollars voucher

News that the villagers were being cheated spread quickly through Ogonbiri. Heads of families who had received the hundredthousand-dollar vouchers rushed back to the school, demanding replacements with the million-dollar vouchers. Sergeant Kokovo, nicknamed "the Sniper," fired warning shots into the air, but the men refused to disperse.

'Give us one million Abazon dollar paper and not one hundred dollar paper!' they chorused as the calmness of the venue started to degenerate into a bedlam. The soldiers shot into the air. The soldiers protected the officials, packed all the documents and escorted the officials to two jeeps parked in the school compound. The tyres of the jeeps had been deflated by irate youths.

'Don't beat the ogas ooo!' Mudiaga and the leader of the youths screamed.

Mudiaga pleaded with the youth leaders to protect the soldiers and officials as they were sequestered in Mudiaga's Primary 4 classroom. Sergeant Kokovo was visibly shaken, aware that if any youth was shot, the soldiers and officials could be lynched by the angry mob. An army pickup truck that served as an escort was used to extract the officials. The youths escorted the soldiers and officials to the truck, which sped off. Once back at the oil company's temporary office, the officials held a meeting.

'This is humiliating!' bellowed Comrade Bamdele. 'How can a one and half legged kid thwart our plan to make millions of Abazon dollars? And that gorilla with speech impairment shouted: "one. Million" a thousand times. He exposed us.'

'C.O Dogo. Let me shoot the two half human boys.' Sergeant Kokovo pleaded.j

'No!' ordered Lt. Dogo. 'Owibo, turn the elders council members against the two disabled rats and their families.'

'Embarrassing!' fumed comrade Bamdele. He turned to Owibo and said: 'You were more senseless than that half-brained gorilla called Uvo which you interpret as the sun.'

'Did you provide an alternative plan?' Owibo asked Bamdele. 'You, mercenary from another state, are not supposed to be working in an oil company located in our state. I will turn my community against you.'

The officials concluded that each family that would relocate would be paid one million Amazon dollars.

Within Ogonbiri community, Mudiaga and Uvo became instant heroes.

'You born better pikin,' became the constant utterance, like the monotonous refrain of a cracked record, anytime indigenes of Ogonbiri saw Mudiaga and Uvo parents.

Chapter Eight

Bulldozers Bulldoze Notable Structures in Ogonbiri Community

As Saturn Oil Company prepared to begin operations in Ogonbiri, they quickly erected a six-office portacabin administrative building. Young people from the community were eager to secure jobs as labourers. Despite the pleas from community heads to delay the beginning of operations for two weeks, the oil company officials rejected and moved on with their plan.

Sundays held special significance when they coincided with market days and the Igbe religious festival, where worshippers danced to the river to offer gifts to the mermaid goddess. On these occasions, worshippers would attend the only church in the community in the morning, dressed in their finest attire. Afterwards, they would join the market crowd and engage in buying and selling. In the evening, a large group would head towards the river to witness the Igbe worshippers dancing. Maidens would carry basins of cassava flour (garri), yam, plantain, and, in this special case, two goats. These offerings were thrown into the river to appease the deities Olokun and Osulu, near the large tree where Mudiaga used to watch and admire the fish. Inside Eloho's large provisions shop, Esama and Eloho's friend discussed their concerns about the new oil company's plans to demolish the market. Eloho already had a four-year-old daughter with Orode and had been a good stepmother to Uvo. Orode had built his own house in the resettlement area, and Peregba's new home was nearby. Orode had recently moved into his completed house with Eloho. Since Orode often traveled for his artisanal refinery business, Peregba played a fatherly role for the baby girl. Peregba would regularly visit Eloho when Orode was away. Esama and Eloho also worried that the oil company's activities might destroy the long stretch of ponds at the riverbank and the ones dug in the swamp, which were usually harvested during seasonal floods.

Peregba kept a grasscutter and snail farm in his backyard. Pere, like many households by the riverbank, was fascinated by the local wildlife. Unlike goats, which were considered domestic animals, fish, antelopes, and grasscutters were also seen as domesticated here. These animals freely roamed the community and returned to their pens at night. Owners wouldn't release them daily but ensured their children cut grass for them to eat. Additionally, they were fed rotten potato and yam peels, and plantain peels. This unique practice of keeping these animals was exclusive to this community, protected by the water goddess.

There had been a few instances where thieves attempted to steal grasscutters or antelopes when most residents were out for the day and children were at school. However, these thieves would become disoriented and wander aimlessly within the community until evening, still clutching the stolen animals. This phenomenon, known as "gerrymandering" by the community, stopped all attempts at theft. Since thieves were guaranteed to be caught, market sellers weren't even worried about leaving their wares unattended.

Local folklore suggests the water mermaid (Olokun) and a community deity (Osulu) protect Ogonbiri from thieves. Youths traditionally dive into the river to retrieve offerings thrown to appease these deities. One year, after youths collected offerings, they found themselves unable to leave the water - the items stuck to their bodies. The Igbe leader had to intervene and appease the deity before they were released. This incident, along with past interventions by the community deity, solidified the belief in their protective powers. As at when they went to give their offerings, the Igbe worshippers had pleaded with their goddess to protect the food items being offered to her. There were also spates of stealing in the communities and worshippers of the deity appeased the deity for protection and the community members were protected. This unique, communal way of life faces extinction as relocation to New Ogonbiri looms.

On a Sunday morning, while churchgoers and Igbe worshippers attended services, the rumbling of bulldozers shattered the peace. Soldiers had arrived three days prior and set up camp. Now, on the outskirts of the village, the bulldozers began demolishing structures. The same devastation unfolded in Ziribiri village.

Church services ended abruptly, replaced by cries and wailing as people scrambled to salvage belongings. Mudiaga, alarmed, informed his parents that their home, the one he saw during his vision quest with the golden fish, was being bulldozed. He urged them to relocate, but his father remained hopeful that the company would grant the community's two-week extension request.

Mudiaga, recalling a Friday lesson, remembered that the following day was Independence Day and the school would be celebrating. He reflected on the concept of independence, learning how it liberated Abazonians from potential eternal enslavement by the

British. Independence, he thought, meant freedom of expression and protection from oppression.

At precisely 1:00 PM, a harsh reality unfolded. The bulldozers began demolishing the market, the church, the Igbe shrine, and the ancestral worship hall. The very foundations of their community life were being destroyed.

PART 2

Chapter Nine

Drilling of Oil Well in Ogonbiri

Saturn Oil Company began drilling in both Ogonbiri and Ziribiri communities. While an oil well and a gas glare cone were drilled in Ogonbiri, only an oil well was drilled in Ziribiri community. They constructed a new primary school in Ogonbiri to replace the demolished one. Comrade Bamdele assured the community that a secondary school would be built soon, alleviating the concern of

Mudiaga's long commute for his education after primary school. Peregba particularly valued this promise, as Mudiaga would soon complete his primary school education.

The oil rigs were set up, and pipelines were dug to connect the crude oil to the flow station and export terminal in Torugbene. Within six months, oil was flowing through the pipelines. During this period, Owibo was, however, engaged in corruption. He sold job slots meant for Ogonbiri residents to outsiders, categorized as "ghost workers," who then paid him a kickback of 40% of their salary. This violated the agreement made at the town hall meeting for Ogonbiri youth to fill junior staff positions. Despite this, a surge of money temporarily flowed into the community. Young women were also lured into prostitution with oil workers for large sums. Peregba, wary of this trend, urged the elders to formalize an agreement guaranteeing junior staff positions for Ogonbiri and Ziribiri residents.

However, after six months in the new community, relocated families faced new challenges. Mudiaga was surprised to find the land covered in concrete, offering no soil or marshland for his usual activities of digging worms and fishing. The river was also a significant distance away (around five kilometres), making it impossible for Peregba to build a fishpond as he had before. Additionally, the houses were built close together, unlike their previous homes.

A contractor drilled a borehole for the community, but the water flow stopped after just a month. Residents were then forced to wake up early and queue for water. The situation worsened when the borehole water became muddy in the second week and completely stopped flowing in the third month. With no other option, the community had to return to fetching water from the distant river. Eloho now had two daughters and had gained some weight. Orode had built a successful business empire, with a three-bedroom flat, a five-room block with a living room close to the riverbank, and a store run by Eloho in front of the compound. The store, conveniently located near the jetty, sells provisions and household items like plates, cutlery, and pots.

'My angel Gabriel wants me to give him a boy,'
'You and Orode as your angel Gabriel,' laughed Esama.
'Yes o! My angel Gabriel wiped tears from barrenness and homelessness from my life.'
'But he has a son. He wants Uvo to have a brother.'
'You should understand na. He wants a complete son. Just like Mudiaga's younger brother.'
'Yes ooo! I call Uvo my first child and he respects me so much. I pray Uvo's best friend finally has two complete legs,' Eloho stated with a frown.

'Your angel has money. Can't he take Uvo to hospital so that doctors can operate his brain and make him talk well?'
'Doctors said there is nothing they can do to correct Uvo's inability to talk well.'

"My husband told me that he told your husband to stop his local refinery business since the army has burnt many refineries down and he promised he will stop. But he refused to stop," Esama noted.

'I have also told my angel Gabriel. I told him that what I make from my store and the rent he collects from his three houses are enough for us to live our lives and train our children.'

Eloho pointed out that her husband is a very stubborn man and he bribes soldiers and the Navy; so, he is never harassed. She added that he has assured her that once he completes the building of two new hostel blocks in the university in Ododo city, he will stop the refinery business.

'Let us hope he will stop. My husband is still working as a labourer in that yeye oil company. But he will soon complete his building, a shop built with planks for me by the bank of River Ona. I will pack my store there.'

Esama said she wondered why her husband refused to partner with Orode in his refinery business. Peregba kept telling his wife that the business is too dangerous.

'Your husband na fear fear man,' Eloho noted. 'Uvo and his father are stone hearts.'

Esama recalled that after her husband's brutal treatment in the hands of soldiers when he was a youth activist in Eko, he has learnt to avoid anything that will lead to his breaking the law and his arrest. 'You don hear the news?' Eloho asked her friend.

'No! Which news? Esama gawked at her friend in expectation of the news.

'That woman who gave birth to two children for my former husband said the children belong to another man. She said my former husband cannot impregnate a woman.'

'Thank God, you're free from that bondage called marriage,' Esama told her friend. 'Oh,I forgot to tell you that matron Etobo died last month. Her second leg was cut and she was completely blind before she went home to rest.'
Did you attend her burial ceremony?'
'Yes! My husband and I attended the burial.'

Chapter Ten

Mudiaga Family's Returns to Kpakiama Fishing Community

Less than a year after relocating to New Ogonbiri, Esama suggested a trip to Kpakiama for their annual fishing expedition. Esama had now given birth to four children, two boys and two girls. Her third child, a healthy baby boy, was named Afure, meaning "spotless white" by Peregba.

However, the environmental impact of oil exploration was evident in both communities. The natural water flow in the creeks of Oloibiri State had been disrupted by the uprooting of trees to lay crude oil pipelines. This not only made fish scarce in the swamps, streams, and rivers but also dried up the stream that Ogonbiri families relied on for fresh water. The gas flare cone was built where the large tree, the source of the stream, once stood. Additionally, the stream where women and children used to collect fish during the dry season had vanished entirely. Fresh fish became a luxury in the New Ogonbiri Community.

The academic calendar of the students was also greatly disrupted since the new Primary school was not roofed. Parents and pupils were told that Owibo and members of the elders committee applied for an upward review of the two blocks of classroom contracts. Owibo insisted that the upward review must be paid before the roofing of the two blocks of classrooms can commence. Due to the insistence of Owibo, the new academic session began in April of a new year instead of September of the previous year. So, the pupils lost two terms. In February, Peregba's family travelled to Kpakiama. The family was very happy since the two young children are physically fit and mentally stable. Ese and Mudiaga were very close to Afure, the boy and Ovo, the girl.

The family hoped to spend two weeks in Kpakiama fishing community. The settlement is a point where about four rivers converge and where people come to fish. While some of the people are fishing, there is a set of women that specialize in drying the different species of fish caught.

The situation in Kpakiama mirrored their own. As they entered the community, Esama, noticing two flare cones, remarked,

'Oil Company must have come to kill all the fish in Kpakiama.'

Peregba, ever optimistic, countered that the women of Kpakiama would benefit – the heat from the flare cones would be perfect for drying fish, particularly kpokpogarri.

While Peregba might have been hopeful, Esama's premonition held true. The fish catch had significantly decreased. The digging of pipelines had altered the natural water flow, reducing the water channels. Additionally, the removal of large trees along the riverbanks to make way for pipelines, flare cones, oil wells, and flow station buildings had eliminated the natural ponds that formed during the dry season. The rivers themselves were completely dried up.
Esama also observed that the once-shaded areas where children played were now barren wastelands, resembling a Sahara Desert. The large trees had been cleared for pipelines that crisscrossed Kpakiama and its surroundings. The remaining trees were being cut down for timber and used as firewood in local creek refineries.

On the first night, Mudiaga, now a primary six student, reminisced about how just five years ago, Kpakiama was a dense forest with abundant water flowing through its four intersecting rivers. Now, the landscape was a desolate reminder of its former beauty. Esama learned that an oil spill had occurred three months before the fishing season, contaminating the rivers. Everyone at the fishing expedition knew this would significantly affect the catch.

Esama and Peregba saw sludge coating the banks of the large lake and at the roots of trees along the rivers. Lament filled the air as fishermen witnessed the devastation. Peregba showed his children oil floating on the water's surface.

Beyond clean water scarcity being a problem to the itinerant fishermen, firewood was also a problem. The very trees they needed were being cut down, depriving the fish of crucial food sources. This deforestation had also caused partial desertification of the oncelush mangrove forest. Mudiaga recalled seeing packs of monkeys, chimpanzees, and various birds during previous visits. Now, the nighttime soundscape was eerily silent.

The arrival of the oil industry had undeniably disrupted the delicate balance between humans and their natural habitat. Everyone wondered about the fate of the pristine environment Peregba grew up in, and where the creatures that once thrived in the trees had migrated. Monkeys, squirrels, snakes, and birds of all sizes were nowhere to be seen. Observing these creatures, a pastime for some fishermen who brought hunting guns, was no longer part of the experience.

Mudiaga questioned whether his father would ever return to the fishing camp. Fish were scarce, and many people now preferred building their own ponds to the traditional two-week fishing expeditions with meager returns.

The social aspect of this biannual event, once a cornerstone of community life, was fading away. The schools built for children accompanying their parents were falling apart. The roofs had been dismantled, their planks repurposed as firewood for cooking and smoking the few fish caught.

Large fish, which once found shelter beneath the tree roots, had migrated to deeper brackish waters near the ocean – a territory teeming with crocodiles and pythons. Fear of these predators deterred fishermen, as many had lost their lives to these dangers. Some of the large snakes were identified as African anacondas.
Peregba recognized that this once vibrant communal fishing tradition, an important festival for these communities, was rapidly disappearing. It marked the death of a social fishing expedition. After two days in Kpakiama with virtually no fish caught, Peregba was forced to return to New Ogonbiri with his family.

'Oil Companies have killed Kpakiama's annual fishing community,' Peregba lamented.
****

The first rains brought disaster to the newly built Ogonbiri community. Due to a lack of drainage and blocked waterways leading to the main river, the town became flooded with mud. Ironically, the oil well and gas flare sites remained unaffected.
However, a strange phenomenon occurred. Water began to gush from beneath the gas flare cone despite the intense heat. The foreign engineer was baffled – shouldn't the heat dry up any underground water?

Following community concerns, Owibo was advised to consult traditional healers of the Igbe religion and the priest who worshipped the uprooted "Tree of Life." They explained to Owibo that the water mermaids residing under the tree were enraged by the desecration of their sacred spot with the gas flare cone. To appease them, the priests recommended planting replica trees at various locations throughout the new town.

'Forget these people's primitive religion,' the American head of the oil company scoffed.

Zikiye, another resident, offered a different perspective. He believed Neptune and Poseidon, the Greek and Roman gods of water, were now residing under the uprooted tree and were flooding the communities in retaliation.

'They are now vomiting water non-stop in order to flood Ziribiri and Ogonbiri communities,' Zikiye asserted.

The constant gushing of water forced the company to dismantle and relocate the gas flare cone at significant expense. The original spot where the Tree of Life stood once again became a source of fresh, clean drinking water for the community. Interestingly, two new trees even began to sprout where the gas flare cone had been removed.

<h1 style="text-align:center">Chapter   Eleven</h1>

Zikiye Teaches Mudiaga Drawing

Mudiaga was now in J.S.S 3, honing his skills in drawing and visual arts. Mr Zikiye, Mudiaga's primary school teacher had graduated with a good degree in Political Science and was now teaching temporarily at the secondary school while hoping to land an administrative job at Saturn Oil Company.

Zikiye had always been captivated by the power of photography and fine art to expose social ills and corruption. He saw the potential in Mudiaga's innocent art to bring global attention to the environmental and social injustices plaguing the oil-producing community of Ogonbiri. However, Zikiye questioned whether Mudiaga, at such a young age, possessed the necessary maturity for the role of a committed artist.

Zikiye envisioned collabourating with Mudiaga, or even using him as the focal point, to draw international attention to the environmental pollution and injustice ravaging their communities. He remembered two influential books recommended by his Fine Arts teacher: *The Fine Artist as a Rebel* and *The Artist as the Eye of Society*. There might have been a third, titled *Fine Art/Photocopy as Crusader* or *Purposeful Fine Art/Photography*. While Mudiaga might not be able to read them yet, Zikiye believed he could grasp how art can raise awareness about pressing community issues.

Zikiye saw Mudiaga as a potential voice for the oil-producing communities of Eko and Ogonbiri. To inspire him, Zikiye asked Mudiaga to recall specific incidents: the soldiers driving students from the primary school, the bulldozers demolishing the school building, and the uprooting of the community's "Tree of Life" by a caterpillar.

'I want you to draw anything about the incidents,' Zikiye told Mudiaga

Mudiaga responded by sketching the chaos when his pregnant mother fell and spilled food, pepper stinging her eye in the commotion. Another drawing depicted the bulldozing and uprooting of the "Tree of Life," the community's water source, which was later replaced by a gas flare cone. Mudiaga even captured a scene from when he discovered his father was about to be cheated out of nine hundred thousand Abazon dollars.

He also drew a series on the neglected state of the roads, contrasting it with doctored photos on social media that portrayed them as newly paved. Zikiye gifted Mudiaga his old phone. Despite the challenge of finding electricity to charge it, Mudiaga was thrilled to have a phone. Zikiye used the phone to show Mudiaga real photos from the past three years, exposing the discrepancy between budgeted road repairs in Eko Local Government Area (LGA) and their true, dilapidated state.

'The gully by the bridge before Ziribiri has always been a death trap,' Zikiye told Mudiaga.

Mudiaga recalled being terrified whenever the vehicle he boarded to Ofodo crossed that bridge. As it descended into the cavernous pit, the vehicle would struggle to extricate itself from the pit. Both sides of the road were swampy, and the bridge railings had been stolen. Collisions between trucks and smaller vehicles often resulted in cars or buses plunging into the river, with tragic consequences. Mudiaga hopes to paint this perilous spot. Finally, Mudiaga's artwork culminated in a portrayal of mothers and children sweating profusely under the gas flares while drying kpokpogarri.

'Well, you have to draw and draw and redraw these four drawings before you come up with the one you feel is very good.' Zikiye told Mudiaga. 'The next thing we will do is to look for outlets that I will send the drawings to. I know there will be some online outlets where you can upload the drawings into. I will look for such outlets.'
Mudiaga became preoccupied with the painting by improving on the artwork. Zikiye bought two big drawing books which Mudiaga used to improve on his drawings.

Mudiaga's father, Peregba, sensed his son was being influenced. He invited Zikiye to their home on Saturday with Mudiaga present. Peregba offered Zikiye a traditional welcome: a bottle of ogogoro (local liquor) with one hundred Abazon dollars and a kola nut. After pleasantries, Peregba spoke bluntly.

'My life is that of a poor man because I made mistakes. I fought oil company bosses in Eko and I was sacked. Now, the same company has come to Ogonbiri and they don't want to give me a good job because of my past.'

Peregba declared he didn't want his children fighting the government or Saturn Oil Company again.

'What you are telling Mudiaga to do is to fight the government or oil Company. I want him to stop these drawings. He already has enough problems with his deformed leg.'

'I want to sell the paintings for Urukpe online and he will make big money,' Zikiye told Peregba.

'No. I don't want wahala. Mudiaga must stop the drawings.' Peregba riveted his gaze at Zikiye and asked: 'Who gave Mudiaga the new name Urukpe?'

'It's me. It means light in our language. God wants him to be light to the community by documenting what is happening in the community through drawings while also making money.'

'If the oil company and government know that he is exposing them, they will just kill him. He is my first son.'

'We will not take the drawings to report to the police. He is enjoying it and we are going to use the drawing to enter for competition and if he wins he can use the money he will make to pay for an operation on his leg and finance his university education. Mudiaga and I are using verbal weapons to expose the ills of the oil companies to our communities. Have you not heard the aphorism: "The pen is mightier than the sword"? Verbal or mental weapons are better than militants' military grade weapons in the fight for an egalitarian society.'

'I don't want soldiers to call my son a militant and the soldiers will arrest and kill my son.'

'Fear fear man!' Esama hollered as she entered the sitting room from one of the bedrooms. 'Young man, sell the pictures. We need money.' Esama riveted her gaze at her husband and said:
'Work with Owibo. You refused. Work with Orode in his petrol company, you refused because of fear fear. How can you continue to fear the cow and also fear its shit?'

Peregba was shocked by his wife's reaction. 'Me, fear fear man?' he asked his wife rhetorically.

'Yes. You're from this community. Make money from the oil God gave this community. See our house! Chairs are broken. Ceiling fan is spoilt. We do not have good food to eat. 14 inches television spoilt. No fridge. No generator. Let Mudi with his one and half leg fight the fight you could not fight with your complete two hands and complete two legs!'

'Is this my wife?'

'No. Na your sister!'

Zikiye tried to calm the frayed nerves between husband and wife. He then said that Mudiaga's mother is correct in her assessment of her husband.

'There is the need for little rebellion against the corruption and flagrant stealing taking place in the oil-rich Eko local government area in general and Ogonbiri and Ziribiri oil communities in particular. I'm from Ziribiri. I cannot get a job in Saturn oil Company but Owibo the secretary of Ogonbiri elders' council and Bamdele, who is a non-indigene, are giving non-indigenes jobs. They sell the jobs. Mudi is at the nodal head of the mild rebellion against our devastated environment and poverty that the oil company has brought upon us.'

For the first time, Peregba saw sparkles of fire in his wife's eyes. He suspected her anger stemmed from the wealth displayed in Eloho's home, which made her accuse him of indolence and pusillanimity. 'I will not do refinery business just to please you,' Peregba told his wife.

'Uncle, I don't support that illegal and dangerous business myself. It is stealing.'

'Who tell you it is stealing? It is our oil. Orodoe is taking the oil in his land to do petrol and sell,' Esama responded.

'Young man, I will think about this ritual you want to use my first son who is disabled for. I will discuss with my son and give you a reply tomorrow,' Peregba told Zikiye.

'Is a twisted leg a great disability?' Zikiye asked Peregba. 'Go and read about Dr Stephen Hawkins, Steve Wonder, Bradly Walker, Marlese Matlan and Talph Brawn and you will know what is called disability. Read about their monumental achievements and you will know what I mean by ability in disability,' stated Zikiye and he stood up and left.

That evening, Peregba confronted his wife about her sudden interest in oil money. He reminded her that when oil was discovered in Ogonbiri, she'd advocated for relocating due to her negative experiences in Eko, their former oil-producing community. Esama explained that Batowei's mother, once her friend, no longer greeted her after Owibo, the secretary of the elders' council, struck it rich with the oil company. Esama felt bitter that the oil company wouldn't help with Mudiaga's leg surgery, while Comrade Bamdele, an outsider, held the power to deny them assistance. Peregba then turned to Mudiaga and asked if he understood the risk of arrest for his drawings.

'Daddy, I enjoy drawing, fishing and craft work with pa Oyegba. I enjoy all of them. I'm not happy the oil company did not help to repair my leg when I was a baby. Daddy, I will not stop drawing because of the fear of the Oil Company that did not bring money to operate my leg.'

'My son you're correct,' Peregba responded to his son's utterances. 'I will tell Zikiye tomorrow that he can continue to teach you to draw and to sell your drawings.'

The next day, Zikiye came in the evening and he gave Peregba a note which read thus:

"Comrade Bamdele, the Community Relations and Public Relations Officer for Saturn Oil Company and the Olobiri State Ministry of

Education, announced last week that the company has decided to sponsor a traditional wear fashion show, poetry competition, and a crafts and art competition for secondary school students at Ogonbiri Model Secondary School. Prize money has been allocated to each category."

'Okay ooo! Now, I join my son to tell Saturn Oil Company to develop Ogonbiri and give us good jobs.'
'Motivation is the key to creative success. Mudiaga has the motivation,' Zikiye asserted. He added: 'Uvo and Mudi are audacious boys and success is the child of audacity.'

****

Pa Oyegba, his hair now streaked with gray and his body weakened by age, called for a meeting with Peregba and his sons. Oyegba had always believed Mudiaga and Uvo to be half-brothers, assuming a woman delivered Uvo to Peregba before his marriage. Despite Mudiaga's physical limitations and Uvo's own challenges, everyone in the community admired the boys' business sense and dedication to their education. Pa Oyegba's intention was to convince Mudiaga and Uvo to assist him after school.

When Peregba, Mudiaga, and Uvo arrived at Oyegba's workshop, Uvo promptly fetched an extra bench from the storage area for Peregba. Peregba reminisced about the past decade, when Mudiaga used to spend time at Oyegba's workshop before starting school. Back then, Oyegba was an agile man in his forties. Now, years of hunching over his crafts had caused him to walk with a slight stoop. Oyegba warmly welcomed Peregba and told him that he is proud of his two sons. He added:
'I want your children to come to the workshop when they close from school to work for about three hours. My workshop will soon close down. I need your sons to help me,' Oyegba told Peregba.

'Thank you engineer but you know they will eat and rest when they come from school.'

'I will buy afternoon food for them,' Oyegba assured Peregba. 'Let my children respond to your request,' Peregba stated. 'Over to you Mudiaga and Uvo.'

Mudiaga and Uvo discussed briefly and Mudiaga then responded. 'Thank you our great teacher and engineer. We have heard your request but we will come on Monday to Wednesday and Friday and Saturday. On Thursday, we used to go to set our fish traps and we check the traps on Saturday morning.'

'That is okay. Thank you my children,' responded Oyegba who was overjoyed by the positive response of the children. With their help, he was confident his workshop wouldn't have to close down.

Chapter   Twelve
Orode's Refinery Incinerated by Bombs from Jet Bomber

As Peregba's family sat down for a dinner of cooked cocoyam and palm oil, a bloodcurdling wail shattered the evening peace. The sound grew closer until a woman, her figure wracked with sobs, burst into the house and collapsed at their feet.

'My angel oo. Orode ooo! Airplane has used bomb to kill my Angel,' Eloho wailed.

Eloho, her face contorted in grief, stammered out the tragedy. One of Orode's workers had arrived, breathless, with news of a devastating attack. An Abazon air force jet had bombed Orode's illegal refinery, incinerating everyone there – workers and women buying refined petroleum products alike. The young man claimed he narrowly escaped the inferno while collecting firewood. He also reported that a helicopter had dropped soldiers after the bombing, making the refinery site inaccessible.

Esama, who had just the day before urged Peregba to partner with Orode for the tenth time, sank into despair. She had to relocate to Eloho's home to stay with her during the ordeal.

Meanwhile, Captain Dogo, a covert co-owner of Orode's refinery, advised Orode's younger brother to sell all of his late brother's properties, except the house where Eloho resided. Peregba, fearing the army would seize them anyway, arranged with Dogo and the younger brother to liquidate Orode's assets. The federal government routinely confiscated properties of illegal refinery operators, branding them economic saboteurs.

Eloho and the younger brother knew about four speed boats Orode used for commercial transport, which remained untraceable. They also sold an uncompleted hostel and two other houses. Captain Dogo assured Eloho he would help her access the money from Orode's two bank accounts. The total proceeds from the sales amounted to thirty million Abazon dollars. The family divided the sum: ten million for Eloho, fifteen million for themselves, and five million to settle creditors. Unable to bear living in the house after Orode's burial there, Eloho and her children relocated to another home owned by Orode, closer to Peregba's family.

Peregba nostalgically reminisced his camaraderie with the late Orode.

'Lion heart is gone!' he shook his head in despair. Peregba remembered regular assertion:
'Nothing good is achieved with ease. To be useful the saucepan endures extreme heat.'

Peregba muttered: 'It is the extreme heat that took my friend's life.' He recollected Orode's perpetual plea that in case he dies in the line of his refinery business duty, Peregba should take over the responsibility of his entire family including his wife.

'I should take your wife as my second wife?' Pere asked his friend.
'Yes na, if you want,' responded Orode.

'God forbid. Death is very far from you,' asserted Peregba.

'I have captured fear of death and locked it in a cupboard. I remember a proverb my late father told me about the need to be fearless. Mishaps occur everywhere, close by or far away. The key to life is perseverance.'

A week after the bombing, Captain Dogo finally allowed Orode's younger brother to visit the refinery site. All that remained were ashes and Orode's partially burnt safety boot. These meager remnants were placed in a coffin and buried in the bedroom Orode once shared with Eloho. The trauma of the burial left Eloho terrified. She vowed never to spend another night in that house, prompting her move to the house closer to Peregba. There, she had it remodeled into a three-bedroom bungalow.

Captain Dogo, a shady army captain, called Eloho, propositioning her to be his lover in exchange for protection. Eloho flatly rejected his advances. Meanwhile, Orode's younger brother, already married with two concubines, insisted on marrying Eloho based on tradition. Eloho saw this as a ploy to exploit her financially and gain control of Orode's property. To protect herself and provide a father figure for her children, Eloho decided Mudiaga could stay with Uvo in his room at Eloho's house. While Eloho's business boomed, Esama, Peregba's wife, became envious as her children preferred Eloho's delicious meals. Esama also noticed Peregba visiting Eloho, though these were innocent attempts to comfort his friend's widow.

Eloho, developing feelings for Peregba, gathered her courage and proposed a polygamous marriage. "I want your husband to marry me as a second wife," she told Esama. "It would provide a father figure for my children and security for me. I'll even pay the dowry and all expenses."

'I want your husband to marry me as his second wife so that my children can have a father figure and I can be protected.' Eloho added: 'I will give him money to pay the dowry and the cost for all other expenses.'

'Did I hear you well?' Esama responded.

'Yes.'

'So, you want to marry my husband,' Esama wondered.

'Marry is marry,' asserted Eloho. 'Whether I marry uncle Peregba or uncle Peregba marry me, marry is marry.'

Esama was disheartened by this development. But Esama asked her friend:
'Hope my husband will not touch you if I agree to your request?'
"He must touch me na. My body isn't firewood," Eloho countered.
When Esama discussed the development with Ese, her elder daughter, Ese was nonplussed. Ese told her mother:
'Decide for yourself, although I don't like it.'

Esama told her friend that it is up to her to convince her husband. If her husband agrees, she, Esama, has no objection.

This unconventional arrangement raised eyebrows in Ogonbiri. Rumors swirled that Eloho was now practicing polyandry, with Orode fathering her daughters and Peregba offering emotional support and acting as a father figure to all three children. Esama has remained nonplussed by the rumour that Eloho and Peregba might be intimate since Esama and her husband benefit financially from Orode. Orode has never suspected Eloho of cheating on him; neither has Peregba developed affection for his best friend's wife. However, when Orode died, Peregba wondered what role he had to play with regard to taking care of Orode's wife and the three children. Peregba was not surprised when his wife told him of Eloho's proposal.

'I will still take care of Eloho and her children as I used to before my friend died but marry my late friend's wife? NEVER!' asserted Peregba.

Then, the incredible happened.
Eloho brought her relatives and came to Peregba's place after booking an appointment a week prior. Eloho's elder brother opened the discussion after initial pleasantries.

'We have come to marry from your home,' he said.
'Ese is too young to get married,' Peregba responded.
It is not your daughter we came to look for her hand in marriage. It is you that we have come to marry.'
'Me? How?'

'My sister Eloho wants to marry you so that you can protect her children, her business and her personality.'
'Give me two days,' Peregba responded.
When Peregba asked his wife, Esama did not show any emotion.
Ultimately, Peregba agreed. Eloho provided the funds needed for the marriage ceremony. All the children from both mothers were ecstatic about the marriage.

When Mudiaga told Zikiye of how Uvo's stepmother married his father, he blurted out:
'Wonders shall never end! Is Ogonbiri now a matriarchal society? When did women start marrying men in Ogonbiri? Uvo's foster mother is an archetype of Aphrodite. She is too elegant, too urban and too fashion-savvy.'

'Hope you're not abusing my second mother?' Mudiaga asked Zikiye. 'No. Not at all. I'm complimenting her,' responded Zikiye. Hope your father's new wife won't be his Achilles heel.'

Mudiaga did not understand a word of what Zikiye had been saying.

Chapter   Thirteen

The Fashion, Poetry, Art and Craft Competition in Ogonbiri Model Secondary School

The graduation ceremony for the first graduating class of Ogonbiri Model Secondary School's senior students and the third graduating class of junior students promised to be a memorable event. Peregba and Esama beamed with pride – their daughter Ese was graduating from senior secondary school, while Mudiaga was graduating from junior secondary school. The management of Saturn Oil Company, the school's founder, also wanted to play a prominent role in the ceremony.

The school had opened its doors to students in JSS 1 (Junior Secondary 1) and SSS 1 (Senior Secondary 1). Ese and other students from Ogonbiri transferred to Ogonbiri Model Secondary School as SSS 1 students.

After two meetings with the teachers, it was decided that the students would showcase their artistic talents through displays of arts and crafts, drama performances, and poetry readings of their own compositions. Then, Owibo and Comrade Bamdele, accompanied by two soldiers as escorts, arrived to inspect the school's renovations, which included a new roof and paint job. They explained that the Managing Director of Saturn Oil Company International, headquartered in Houston, Texas, would be visiting the oil facilities in Olobiri State. Comrade Bamdele had learned that Dr. Howard, the Managing Director, was a lover of arts and crafts. His presence at the student exhibition and poetry reading would be a fantastic opportunity to showcase the creativity of both the students and teachers.

A month into the arts, crafts, and poetry competition, Mudiaga approached Uvo, who was still clad in black mourning clothes for his father. Recognizing Uvo's essential role in their success in the crafts competition, he implored him to let them put together the craft items they will present for the competition.

'So, how many items are you taking to the competition venue?'Mudiaga asked Uvo.

'Many. Fish trap. Fish. Woman trap. Broom. Big. Small. Hook. Garri sieve.'

'Plenty o,' observed Mudiaga. 'Uncle Zikiye said we should make them beautiful oo!'

'We. Paint,' noted Uvo. 'We. Take. 3, 3.'
'Yes, take three for each item because uncle Zikiye said some guests can buy an item. Let me bring one Arts book and we select colours to use. I buy paint and we paint after we complete the crafts.'
Together, Uvo, Ese, and Mudiaga selected colours for the crafts. Mudiaga then bought the paint, and they began their work. Each broom received a coat of blue, yellow, and brown.

Zikiye also provided guidance on the colors for Mudiaga's final artwork. For the painting depicting the incident at school when pepper was thrown in Mudiaga's mother's eyes, Zikiye suggested using gray as the background color. In contrast, Zikiye advised using red for the backdrop of "The Tree of Life" painting, uprooted by a gas flare cone. At the bottom of the painting, Mudiaga was instructed to write: "Uprooting the Tree of Life with a Gas Flare Cone." Due to the commotion at the school, Zikiye decided the caption should be changed to "Replace School with Crude Oil."

Finally, for the artwork representing the unbuilt roads, Mudiaga used black as the background colour.

'There will be a fashion parade where traditional attire will be displayed by students to showcase our different languages and cultures in Oloibiri state. There will be an arts and crafts exhibition. Here, drawings, and crafts like broom, traps, hooks and sieves will be showcased by the students. Finally, there will also be a poetry presentation, traditional fashion display and song rendition by students too.'

A wave of excitement swept through the students when Zikiye announced the prize money for the competition winners. The prospect of winning money further motivated many students to participate in the exhibition.

'Mudi, me, you and Uvo will form our group with you as group leader,' Ese told her younger brother.

Ese, now a stunning young woman in SSS 3, had become a surrogate mother figure to her three younger siblings and Eloho's children. With Esama focusing on her thriving business, Ese had taken over cooking duties at home. Determined to see her eldest daughter attend a university even if finances were tight, Esama had encouraged Ese to pursue fashion design since her promotion to SSS 1.
'You will work in the oil company and marry an engineer in the oil company too,' Esama always told her daughter.

'Me, I will read poetry and shakara with my mummy wrapper and head tie,' Ese noted as the three of them put final touches to their preparation.

'Me, I will show my drawings and I will also show our crafts with Uvo,' stated Mudiaga.

'We. Must. Take. First,' Uvo said with a smile.
They submitted their list of activities for the competition.

The school grounds received a makeover. Two large, brand-new canopies were erected. Both school buildings were repainted, and the tables and chairs were adorned with white and pink cloths. Two canopies were designated for guests, while a third one opposite them, with benches at the back, was for the competitors. An enclosure at one end of the third canopy provided a changing area for the dance troupe and fashion group. Palm trees were trimmed, and an interior decorator transformed the entire compound with beautiful decorations. The event was scheduled to take place from 10:00 AM to 1:00 PM on a Thursday in August, marking the start of the long summer vacation.

News reached the management of Saturn Oil Company that the governor of Olobiri State would accompany Dr. Howard on a visit to the Eko flow station and gas plant in the morning before attending the graduation ceremony at Ogonbiri Model Secondary School. In anticipation of their arrival, the state commissioner for works ordered the refurbishment of the road from Ododo to Eko. Crews cut back overgrown trees that were obstructing the road and cleared both sides for better visibility. Shantytowns, mud houses, and illegal *ogogoro* distilleries lining the roadside were masked with large tarpaulins emblazoned with messages like:

'Welcome the best governor of the Republic of Abazon.'
'Welcome Managing Director (Global) of Saturn Oil Company'
Stolen rails on the bridges along the Ododo-Eko road were replaced and painted. Students from primary and secondary schools across the state were transported to the Ododo-Eko road,

where they were each given a small Abazon flag to wave as the governor and Mr. Howard's convoy passed.

Meanwhile, tension rose as local youths in Ogonbiri and Eko planned a peaceful protest demanding inclusion in the amnesty program they had been excluded from. Additionally, Peregba, along with other casual workers of the oil company in Ogonbiri, intended to stage a peaceful protest for their conversion to permanent staff. Peregba, with his experience from previous protests in Eko, volunteered to lead the casual workers' demonstration.

However, the Directorate of State Security (DSS) intercepted intelligence suggesting plans by militant youths to attack the governor's convoy and disrupt the graduation ceremony. They also received information about a potential violent demonstration by casual oil company workers in Eko and Ogonbiri, aimed at pressuring the managing director to order the conversion of casual workers to permanent staff.

'My head used to swell and I will feel like I'm floating in the air anytime Mr Zikiye praises me,' Mudiaga told his elder sister, Ese. 'Just for that reason, Mr Zikiye should continue to praise you till you finish S.S.S. 3,' Ese replied playfully.

'No! I don't want to go further after this J.S.S. 3. What will I do with the S.S.S. 3 result?'

'You can get scholarship to travel to America for studies and your leg can be operated there,'

'Ese the dreamer!' Mudiaga laughed.
The day arrived, and spectators lining the streets of Ogonbiri noticed a smaller-than-usual convoy. Comrade Bamdele

represented Dr. Howard at the ceremony, while the Commissioner for Education stood in for the governor. Due to these last-minute absences, the planned protests by the youths and casual workers failed to materialize.

The ceremony began with a welcome address from Mr. Zikiye, the acting principal. This was followed by the reading of the governor's speech by the commissioner for education. Finally, Comrade Bamdele addressed the audience, highlighting the oil company's development efforts in host communities like Eko and Ogonbiri. He also explained why gas flaring hadn't ceased in these areas.

'We listened to the yearning of the women who do business with the heat and fire of the gas flaring sites. That is why we did not reinject the gas.'

Everyone knew, however, that the real reason Saturn Oil Company didn't reinject the gas was the high cost involved.

The first event was the fashion parade. Ese, clad in her native attire, was clearly the favourite among the female contestants. Eloho, now pregnant with Peregba's child, had helped Ese dress up, applying light makeup and guiding her on a catwalk on the grassy field. Ese wore a beautiful brown double wrapper with a matching headtie, complemented by a white blouse, silver jewelry, a brown handbag, and even a matching brown phone. When she appeared wearing stylish brown designer eyeglasses, the Master of Ceremonies (MC) boomed:
'Here comes Miss Ogonbiri. No. Miss Olobiri state!
Here comes a classic example of black beauty and brain.'
Eloho, visibly pregnant at six months, sat beside Esama and other women. She looked stunning in a brown maxi gown with a matching bag and white headtie.

'You like fashion sha oo!' Esama told her husband's second wife.'
'My late husband always wanted me to dress well. My angel Gabriel will always tell me: "Show them fashion, my queen. Chop my money through your dine dressing," Eloho told Esama.

Three other female students participated in the fashion parade, all showcasing traditional wear. However, Ese stole the show. Many officials showered her with crisp Abazon dollar bills, while others offered envelopes. Inside one envelope, Ese found a note with a phone number:

'Call me soon and you will spend the weekend in the Presidential hotel, Ododo with me.'

Another note read: 'Call me and let me wipe poverty from your family forever,' Ese chuckled when she read the notes.

Following the fashion parade, it was time for the poetry reading. The Ogonbiri Model Secondary School students were surprised to hear the MC call Batowei to the stage. Batowei had only attended the school as a JSS 1 student before transferring to a prestigious school in Ododo City. However, her father, Owibo, insisted on her involvement in the competition. He even paid Zikiye, the acting principal, twenty thousand Abazon dollars to write a poem for his daughter and coach her on delivery. Batowei, dressed in a yellow blouse and trousers, stood before the audience to recite her poem titled "Rotten".

Rotten
When meat or fish is getting
rotten, It is the head that first gets
rotten.
If the head of a society is corrupt and rotten

Citizens of the society and its citizens will remain poor.
Poverty and misery will be the lot of the society's citizens
Laziness and indecision always set in before breakthrough
The darkest part of the night is before daylight
breakthrough What determines success is ability to struggle
hard till the end.
My parents and fellow students must always struggle till the end.

There was a round of applause after Batowei finished the recitation of her poem. Comrade Bamdele tapped Owibo and said:

'Your daughter did not write that poem. The poem was written to insult and abuse us the elite of the society. Thank God the governor did not come. Your daughter would have been arrested.'

'True oo! And I gave the foolish vice principal plenty of money to write a love poem for my daughter,' noted Owibo with a frown on his face. 'I will deal with him.'

'Your daughter is not supposed to participate because she is not a student of this school,' observed the commissioner for education.
'She did her JSS 1 here,' responded Owibo.
'Why didn't you leave her in this school?'

'My class and level have changed. My daughter cannot attend a public school again. And this public school is in the rural area. NEVER!'

The MC then introduced the next reader, a boy with a disability. He holds the distinction of being the first disabled student to attend secondary school in Eko Local Government Area. He will be reading a poem titled "My Love."

Mr. Zikiye took the microphone from the M.C and applauded Mudiaga as he limped to the podium on his crutches with his poem in his hand:
Here comes Mudiaga the young man who has proved that there is ability in disability.

Here comes Mudiaga, who has shown that academic focus dispels mental disability.

Book head has proved that physical disability is no impediment to academic success.

Book head has shown us that academic success is a prerequisite for financial success.

The genius of Ogonbiri secondary school will in future achieve financial success.
Mudiaga is the Daedalus, the Shakespeare and Michael Angelo of Ogonbiri Secondary School.
Ogonbiri Secondary School will produce the first Dr Stephen Hawking of Abazon republic.
'My head used to swell and I will feel that I'm floating in the air anytime Mr Zikiye praises me,' Mudiaga whispered to his elder sister as he moved gingerly to the podium to read his poem. Mudiaga leaned on his crutches and read his poem after greeting the invited guests.

My love
> *My love is fishing in river Ona with Uvo.*
> *Uvo is my friend and my love*
> *I love eating kpokpogarri and dry fish.*
> *I love Ogonbiri Model Secondary School.*

Ese is my sister
Ese is my love.

My parents and my aunty Eloho are my love
My younger brother and sister are my love
Uncle Zikiye is my role model and my love.
Uncle Zikiye calls me 'ability in disability.
Ability will always overcome disability
> *Love is life.*
> *Life is love*

'This poem reminds me of the song 'One love 'by Bob Marley, the great Jamaican reggae musician. Love is everything,' the M.C noted with a smile. There was a round of applause and the M.C. reminded the audience that the name "Ese" mentioned by Mudiaga in his poem is her elder sister, the model. 'Let us give 'Master Ability in Disability' another round of applause. There was again another round of applause.

'Our next presentation is crafts and drawings, arts and paintings by five groups of contestants."

Uvo, with unwavering determination and encouragement from his father and best friend Mudiaga, secured a spot in JSS 1 at Ogonbiri Model Secondary School. Their group, consisting of Uvo, Mudiaga, and Ese, presented their crafts across from the canopy designated for invited guests.

Their display included fishing hooks, various sized wicker fish traps, garri sieves for both coarse and fine sifting, and short and long brooms – three of each item. As guests approached to inspect the crafts, Uvo served as their enthusiastic explainer. The guests were particularly captivated by the painted decorations.

One woman, especially interested in the brooms, pointed to the short and long ones. Uvo helpfully explained, "Short broom sweeps inside the house. Long broom sweeps outside."

Ese explained the uses of the sieves for both pre-frying and postfrying *garri* to interested guests. Meanwhile, Mudiaga discussed the different types of fish traps used by men and women for fishing. Uvo even elaborated on the specific uses of the three different hook sizes based on the age and depth of the river targeted. Notably, their group's crafts stood out due to their aesthetically pleasing painted designs, attracting more attention compared to the displays of other contestants with fewer and unpainted items. Some officials visiting from Ododo City purchased crafts at prices ten times their market value! Uvo's group, clearly the crowd-pleaser, took first place and the accompanying cash prize.

Finally, it was time for the painting and drawing competition. Although there were three contestants, Mudiaga's artwork received significant attention. His two pieces were displayed side-by-side: the first depicting a monstrous caterpillar uprooting the tree of life in Ogonbiri, and the second portraying women and children struggling under the blazing heat of a gas flare cone while drying kpokpogarri and fish.

Caterpillar uprooting the tree of life   Women and children drying kpokpogarri under gas flare.

Certainly, Mudiaga's paintings were the most beautiful and most attractive. Comrade Bamdele, who studied Fine and Applied Arts before becoming an activist against corruption and oppression, could interpret drawings very well. He perceived his drawings as highly critical of the government and the oil company. These riots by youths can be dismissed as outbursts from young people who are not looking for work and are mainly interested in causing trouble.

Comrade Bamdele then raised an alarm:

'These are political drawings meant to indict and embarrass Saturn Oil Company and the Olobiri state government.' He turned to Mudiaga and warned him sternly, 'Disabled young man, focus on your crafts and leave these paintings or you will land in prison.'

'My son's drawings are truthful!' Peregba shouted.

Zikiye and Mudiaga were astonished by Peregba's temerity.

'Mudiaga's father has finally found his voice.' Zikiye whispered. 'Thank goodness the governor did not come, this disabled boy would have been arrested,' the commissioner for education asserted. 'There must be someone goading you to do these paintings. We will find the person out and punish him.'

Although Mudiaga's artwork was undeniably the best among the three contestants, he was awarded third place.

Before Comrade Bamdele left, he requested to see "Urukpe's" father. He told Mr. Peregba to come see him about converting his position from labourer to a permanent administrative clerk position. Comrade Bamdele bought Mudiaga's artworks and gave him ten thousand Abazon dollars. He instructed his orderly, "Once we get to Ododo city, burn these. Any form of rebellion must be crushed in the bud within all oil-producing communities."

Mudiaga was presented with a new pair of imported crutches. He later discovered that the pair of crutches was quite heavy for him. He also noticed that the two crutches were not the same length.

The winning contestants received half of the prize money. They were told the other half would be given to them when the new session resumed. These prize monies were never paid.

Finally, Mr. Bamdele announced that Saturn Oil Company was collabourating with a top university in the United States of America to award scholarships to students from host communities. He said the program would commence in two years' time. Comrade Bamdele also added that Saturn Oil Company would collabourate with the Commonwealth Scholarship Board to grant Commonwealth scholarships to students from oil-producing communities.

In his closing remarks, Comrade Bamdele commended the management of Ogonbiri Model Secondary School for organizing a successful graduation ceremony for its JSS 3 and SSS 3 graduates. He then raised objections to some of the artworks showcased by some of the students, especially Mudiaga's:

"Some of your students are portraying the state government and the Oil Company in a negative light with their drawings and poetry. We are not bad people at all. Your real enemy is your local chiefs. They take contracts for all the development projects we want to execute in this community, and they just pocket the money.

"I got this appointment from the federal government because I was a staunch critic of the government," Comrade Bamdele told Chief Owibo. "This appointment was given to me to silence me. I'm now a government apologist. My duty is to protect the interests of the government and the oil company. This drawing is supposed to be suppressed by me. The headmaster should ensure that nothing rebellious happens in your school."

"Freudian slip," Zikiye muttered inaudibly. "So, Comrade Bamdele used to be an activist and a rebel. He understands what rebellion against a corrupt government means. Mudiaga is a tiny red pepper. The red pepper is small but can be very irritating to the eye."

In his vote of thanks, the vice principal, Mr. Zikiye, thanked the dignitaries from the state capital for attending the ceremony. He said that Mudiaga and Uvo had demonstrated "ability in disability" through their presentations that day. He added that Ogonbiri Model Secondary School aimed to educate students who were thoughtful and independent-minded, so that they could express their views freely. He concluded with a proverb:

'The possibility of pepper going into the trachea deters nobody from having a meal.'

Mr. Zikiye was later promoted and appointed as the principal of Ogonbiri Model Secondary School.

*****

Pa Oyegba beamed with pride over Mudiaga and Uvo's accomplishments. Two days later, a television crew arrived unannounced to document the activities at the crafts factory and shop. Uvo and Mudiaga weren't informed beforehand; the crew wanted to surprise them. The segment aired on the state television station, catching the eye of the commissioner for arts and culture who became interested in their craftsmanship.

As a result, a modern crafts centre was built in Ogonbiri specifically for Pa Oyegba, Mudiaga, and Uvo. This centre has attracted many children and young people who come to learn various crafts after school. The institute even expanded to include a fashion design section, offering free classes for girls. The Ministry of Youth Development provided workers for the centre, along with a large generator to ensure smooth operation.

Part 3

Chapter   Fourteen

Soldiers Arrest Pipeline Vandals and Oil Thieves

Mudiaga and Uvo set out for a fishing expedition on the banks of the Ona River, planning to travel a long distance. On Saturday evening, they went searching for earthworms to use as bait the next day. Mudiaga rested under a tree while Uvo dug for worms. On Sunday, they walked downriver for about forty-five minutes before finding a good spot to fish with their hooks. Further down,

Mudiaga noticed three speed boats converging on a specific location. He saw drums and numerous twenty-five-liter jerry cans. He wondered what the young men were doing there, especially since he noticed a small inlet or tributary feeding into the river nearby.

Mudiaga was happy to see a tree similar to the one he used to fish from before the arrival of Saturn Oil Company in Ogonbiri. They fished for about four hours, catching over twenty fish of various sizes and species. Mudiaga sold four of the larger fish and brought five home. Esama was thrilled when Mudiaga arrived with the fish. It was later used to make a fresh fish banga soup.

The Sunday fishing expeditions became a regular event for Uvo and Mudiaga. However, Mudiaga continued to notice the young men filling jerry cans at the same spot and loading them onto a speedboat that carried them away.

There had recently been incidents of pipeline vandalism between Ziribiri and the Eko flow station. Captain Dogo commanded the AntiBunkering, Illegal Refinery, and Pipeline Vandalization Task Force across three local government areas. The first group of youths arrested were tortured, and their families spent significant sums of money to secure their release. This second arrest involved a new set of youths who were detained for two weeks, with their loved ones again facing hefty bail costs. The entire community was terrified. There was a pressing need to solve this mystery and clear the name of Ogonbiri, now labeled a hub for bunkering and pipeline vandalism. Captain Dogo informed the youths that anyone with helpful information should report it to Oyegba, the current community chairman.

Then, during their usual fishing trip, Uvo tugged at Mudiaga's T-shirt.

"Oil? Thief? Pipeline breaker?" Uvo whispered, gesturing towards the area where speedboats and dugout canoes used to unload jerry cans and load drums onto speedboats before speeding away. A pipeline ran through the area where the boats and canoes were parked.

"Yes! They're likely oil thieves," Mudiaga confirmed.

Upon returning home, Uvo and Mudiaga reported the incident to Pa Oyegba. Oyegba contacted Captain Dogo. The community leader informed the security forces, who then accompanied Mudiaga back to his fishing spot. Captain Dogo mobilized soldiers to follow Uvo and Mudiaga to the spot on Sunday afternoon. The soldiers hid while Mudiaga and Uvo engaged in fishing as usual. The thieves likely assumed Mudiaga's disability meant he wouldn't suspect them of using the spot as a collection and distribution point for stolen crude oil.

Soldiers Prepare to Attack Oil Thieves

Soldiers surrounded the spot and yelled, "Stop there!" One of the oil thieves fired at the soldiers, injuring a soldier. Two of the oil thieves were also injured in the ensuing firefight. The oil thieves then surrendered.

Reinforcements arrived in speedboats, and the oil thieves were arrested and taken away. They later confessed to bursting pipelines on Saturday evenings and Sundays, taking advantage of the reduced activity on Sundays.

The six captured individuals were not even from the Ogonbiri community. However, they frequented bars in the community, spending money extravagantly.

Community leader Pa Oyegba and Captain Dogo were impressed by Uvo and Mudiaga's alertness. Captain Dogo commended them, bestowing upon them the nickname "Ability in Disabled Youths."
The capture of these individuals significantly reduced tensions within the community, offering a renewed sense of security for the youths.

Chapter Fifteen

Pere Enrolls for SSSE Examination

Motivated by the promise of foreign scholarships, Mudiaga enrolled for his Senior Secondary School Examination (SSSE). In SSS 2, he started saving for the external exam fees. Uvo was then in Junior Secondary School (JSS) 2 and planned to stop school after JSS 3. Eloho, whom Mudiaga calls "Small Mummy," promised to fund his university education.

Many praised Mudiaga's decision and encouraged other youths to follow his example. However, others in the community turned to crime: some engaging in "yahoo yahoo" (cybercrime) and others in illegal oil bunkering by bursting pipelines and stealing crude oil to sell to operators of clandestine refineries.

At the start of the first term, Mudiaga paid his school fees and registration fees for the Senior Secondary School Certificate Examination Board (SSCEB). He met with Mr. Zikiye to redesign his schedule to optimize his study time. This involved arriving early at school (around 7:00 AM) to read before the 8:00 AM assembly, staying back for two hours after the 2:00 PM dismissal, and dedicating additional time on weekends. Despite his studies, he continued to focus on his crafts business.

Many in the community questioned Mudiaga's intense focus on the SSSE exams, unaware of his long-term goal of university admission.
Lost in thought, Mudiaga muttered to himself: "I know I need strong SSS 3 results to even be considered for a scholarship. It's like Animal Farm here - the powerful take our resources while we, the weak, suffer. It's a classic case of 'Monkey dey work, baboon dey chop' (the worker gets nothing, the idler benefits)."

Ese, who had completed secondary school and now taught ladies' fashion design at Oyegba's vocational centre (now owned by the Olobiri State Ministry of Education), stood beside her brother during his soliloquy. "I know one day your leg will be alright," she said. "I saw it in a dream. I don't know how, but I know it will happen."

Despite his concerns about navigating university life with a disability, Mudiaga persevered. He balanced his studies, crafts business, and fishing hobby with additional funds for private lessons in math, English, chemistry, and physics to practice past exam questions with his teachers.

Mudiaga excelled in the mock SSS 3 exam, placing among the top three students in a class of thirty. He earned credits in English, Math, and four other subjects. The principal announced the results at a morning assembly, singling out Mudiaga's success and criticizing the underachieving students.

"Look at Mudiaga," the principal declared. "With one leg, he's among the best students! You, with two legs, hands, eyes, and ears, couldn't even pass English and Math. What will you do if the Commonwealth or Saturn Oil Company scholarship opens up? We won't have enough qualified candidates! So, for those wasting your time like… goatish boys chasing girls, herbalist seekers for overnight riches, resource 'controllers' bursting pipelines and cooking crude oil, girls prostituting with scammers and oil workers… all of you, your future is bleak. This is your last chance to focus on your studies. Cheating won't be tolerated!"

Many students were relieved when the assembly ended. However, some remained defiant. One student even declared his intention to pursue his own illegal refinery and internet fraud schemes.

The announcement for undergraduate Commonwealth and U.S.A. scholarships from Saturn Oil Company was released, targeting students from oil-producing communities. Mudiaga downloaded and printed the application form. One section required completion by the Ogonbiri head, and another required him to attach a printout of his SSCE results. He needed to travel to Ododo City to purchase a scratch card for online result access. The application also requested a recent passport photograph. Ese accompanied him to Ododo City to complete these tasks and submit the application.

Mudiaga's "small mother," Eloho, also encouraged him to apply to Olobiri State University, promising to finance his education there.

After submitting the scholarship application, Mudiaga planned to purchase the Joint Admissions and Matriculation Board (JAMB) form in Ododo City.

Chapter Sixteen

Mudi's Involvement in an Accident

Mudiaga emerged from the foreign scholarship aptitude test feeling confident about his performance. "The office at Saturn Oil Company headquarters where we took the test was freezing!" he told his sister Ese afterward.

"Did Batowei take the test too?" Ese inquired.

Mudiaga confirmed that Batowei was there, even though she was already a second-year university student. Ese wondered why Batowei would bother applying.

Her father will probably pull some strings to get her a spot," Mudiaga explained. "They said there'll be an oral interview for the top scorers."

"You'll definitely get called for the interview," Ese assured her brother.

Mudiaga and Ese, both feeling optimistic, decided to celebrate with a meal at their favourite fast food joint. Afterward, they boarded a rickety bus to return home. The road to their community had been in terrible condition ever since the last rainy season, when floodwaters inundated and partially washed away sections of the road.

Chief Owibo's construction company had been awarded a contract as a temporary fix until a reputable firm could repave the entire road. Their solution was simply to pile sand and gravel at either end of the four bridges between Ododo and Eko. Predictably, these measures failed within two weeks, leaving dangerous dips before and after each bridge.

The washed-out asphalt sections were filled with sand, but the most perilous part remained: a deep valley before the bridge near Ziribiri. Drivers dubbed this spot "Death Valley by the River Ona Bridge." Every vehicle that traversed it sent shivers down passengers' spines. Chief Owibo's jeep approached the valley at high speed. The driver, mistakenly believing he could pass before the rickety sixteen-seater bus with the right of way, failed to yield. Mudiaga, who usually sat near the door for easy exit with his crutches, was flung from the bus when the Prado jeep collided with it. The jeep then toppled onto the bus, tragically crushing most passengers. Those in the back seats were spared the worst.

The most serious injury was to Mudiaga's already-compromised leg. The bus's spare tire, dislodged from the impact, struck and shattered his leg. Ese, who had been sitting beside him, received only minor injuries.

Everyone initially thought Mudiaga dead until he was spotted barely breathing in a nearby bush. Rushed to the health centre, doctors discovered a broken bone in his injured leg. While amputation was initially considered, Peregba insisted on taking his son to a local bone doctor for treatment.

Family members took Mudiaga back to the traditional bone setter who treated his leg when he was a baby. The middle-aged practitioner realigned the broken bones in his injured left leg and bandaged it in its straightened position.

"Because of the accident, the bent leg is now like softened metal; I can adjust it effectively," the bone setter observed.

The bent ankle of his other leg was also straightened and bandaged. "I was still learning the trade when you were brought here twenty years ago," the bone setter explained. "Now, I'm much more experienced. Your leg will heal," he assured Mudiaga, who was in excruciating pain.

Peregba and his two wives were deeply worried about Mudiaga. Esama stayed with him constantly in the village during his treatment. Eloho visited regularly to see both her husband and Mudiaga, whom she affectionately called "my second small husband" (Eloho also referred to Uvo as her "first small husband").

On the day Mudiaga first visited the bone setter, Eloho told him, "Doctor, please take good care of my second small husband." Then, turning to Peregba and Esama, she assured them, "I'll cover any costs the doctor charges.”

Esama and Uvo were overcome with grief and cried openly.
Eloho's business of supplying food to the 5th Battalion of the Abazon Army in Ododo City had made her very wealthy. Lt. Col. Dogo Musa commanded the battalion. Eloho secured Peregba's permission before starting her business of providing cooked meals to soldiers in the creek communities. The army officer treated Eloho with respect as a married woman. She also leased her shop by the riverbank to Esama, who profited significantly as residents from the creek communities purchased food and toiletries there.

"Once you recover, I'll pay for your university education. My business is thriving now," Eloho promised Mudiaga a month into his treatment.

Mudiaga smiled for the first time since the accident. He believed he wouldn't win the scholarship fairly due to the corruption of Owibo and his associates.

The bone setter informed Mudiaga that his treatment would last five months. In the first month, Mudiaga was relieved to see Ese. He had feared she might have died and no one wanted to tell him. The biggest challenges Mudiaga faced in the village were the lack of mobile network coverage for any SIM card and the unreliable electricity supply. The only source of light came from gas flaring about a kilometre away. Mudiaga couldn't understand why such a remote community, so close to an oil well, had no regular electricity or internet access. He also lacked a phone because the one Mr. Zikiye gave him was lost in the accident. Given the financial burden of his treatment and food, he couldn't ask anyone to buy him a new one. Eloho wanted to buy a phone for her foster son, but the bone setter refused, believing calls would distract Mudiaga from his healing.
******

Meanwhile, when Owibo's Prado jeep collided head-on with the rickety Toyota Hiace bus taking Mudiaga and his sister on their way back to Ogonbiri from Ododo City, the impact trapped Owibo's legs beneath the mangled passenger seat. Bystanders used axes to cut through the wreckage and free him. Some onlookers knew that Owibo's construction company had been awarded the contract to repair the damaged section of road where the accident occurred. Unfortunately, his company did a poor job, pocketing the money instead of fixing the road properly.

"Greedy elder!" Zikiye, one of the onlookers, remarked as Owibo was extricated. "See the price of greed. As our elders say, 'Avarice drives the psychotic to endless acquisition of junks.' Owibo thought he was acquiring wealth, but he was just accumulating worthless things."

Owibo screamed in agony as he was pulled from the wreckage. An ambulance arrived to rush him to the Olobiri University teaching hospital. Both legs were bloodied and badly injured.

"Why rush this useless carcass to the hospital?" Zikiye ranted. "He should be buried like a mangy dog!" Owibo was once a respected elder in Ogonbiri, but his actions had turned him into a villain in their eyes.

After cleaning and examining Owibo's legs, the orthopaedic surgeon delivered the grim news: "Both legs must be amputated within a week to prevent gangrene."

"Can't I be flown abroad for treatment? I don't want to lose my legs! I can't be disabled!" Owibo pleaded with the doctor. "No," the doctor replied firmly.

The next morning, Owibo awoke to find himself a double amputee. He was also informed that he had been stripped of his position as Secretary of the Ogonbiri community elders' council. His position had been given to the assistant secretary.
"It's all over," Owibo muttered before succumbing to the effects of the tranquilizers.

Chapter Seventeen

Mudiaga Discharged and Awarded the Foreign Scholarship by Saturn Oil Company

Two months into his expected four-to-five-month stay, the pain in Mudiaga's body and legs had subsided somewhat. However, his spirits sank when rumours spread that the anticipated foreign scholarship, which he felt confident about, had been delayed by six months. The aptitude test results were sent to the Oil Company's headquarters in Texas, USA. Mudiaga worried he'd have to reapply from scratch.

His biggest concern was the possibility of amputation. He questioned why the traditional bone setter wasn't considering taking him to a hospital for the removal of his damaged and twisted left leg.

"Could the bone setter know more than the Western doctors who wanted 200,000 Abazon dollars for the amputation?" Mudiaga pondered.

Whenever he pressed his swollen legs, his fingers sank in like pressing fresh bread. Though he initially worried about worms and pus gushing out of the leg, thankfully, none appeared. Mudiaga clung to this as a flicker of hope.

He knew Uncle Zikiye would be his only source of information on developments in the state capital regarding the scholarship. Mudiaga had scored 240 in his JAMB exam and received an invitation for the Olobiri State University Post-UTME, but he couldn't attend due to the accident.

After four months under the native bone setter's care, Mudiaga was finally discharged. For the first time in his eighteen years, he stood upright, albeit with crutches. He'd begun practicing walking cautiously with both legs a month prior, still using crutches for support. He wasn't allowed to leave until the remaining 100,000 Abazon Dollars was paid. Eloho covered the cost of his treatment. When Mudiaga returned to his village, everyone was amazed to see him walking on two legs, albeit with crutches. He learned his businesses hadn't collapsed; Uvo was running things at Oyegba's workshop. However, the community faced a new challenge: rising water levels from the river were permanently overflowing the banks.

Owibo was informed that the five successful scholarship candidates' names were sent from the company's Houston headquarters to the Saturn Oil office in Ododo City. Mudiaga's name was among the three qualified candidates. However, the company had decided to exclude candidates with disabilities from the scholarship. Owibo ensured his daughter, Batowei, was fourth on the list, confident Mudiaga's disqualification would allow her to take his place.

Mudiaga convinced Ese to accompany him to Ododo City, the capital of Olobiri State, to check on the results of the scholarship aptitude test he took before the accident. He was surprised to find his name listed among the successful candidates from oil-producing communities. He was instructed to come for a medical checkup, followed by an oral interview a week later.

'I passed the aptitude test!' Mudiaga exclaimed.
He then checked the dates for the medical test and the oral interview.
'Shuo! Tomorrow is the last date for the medical examination,' Mudiaga told Ese.

'Just do the medical test today,' Ese advised her brother.

They went to the Saturn oil company clinic. Mudiaga told a middle aged lady who is the matron of the clinic that he was among the shortlisted candidates for medical examination. Mudiaga was shabbily dressed while Ese was well dressed. The matron wondered if Mudiaga truly passed the aptitude test. Luckily, Mudiaga had his Senior Secondary school examination identification card with him.
The matron looked intently at Mudiaga and asked him:
'Are you not the boy with bent leg from Ogonbiri?'
'Formerly bent leg ma,' responded Mudiaga. 'My bent leg is straight now.'

I'm Priye. I was working with late matron Etobo at the maternity home in Ogonbiri when your mother delivered you about twenty years ago. I heard that you died in the accident.'
'I survived. This is my elder sister.'

'Oh, she's a fine young lady now. Look, don't come with crutches for the oral interview or you will be disqualified. The oil company does
not want to sponsor a disabled student.'
Thank you ma,' responded Mudiaga.

'I learnt one widow woman married your father. Is it true that she paid your father's bride price?' Priye riveted her gaze at Mudiaga. Ese and Mudiaga burst into hilarious laughter and responded in unison that it is true.

'Ogonbiri! Wonders shall never end in that community,' Matron Priye observed.

Mudiaga had the medical tests and waited for the results. The results were positive and he travelled back to his community with his sister to prepare for the oral interview.

Members of Mudiaga's family were excited when they heard that Mudiaga would go for the final oral interview for the award of foreign scholarship the following week. Eloho invited Mr. Zikiye and she gave him some money to buy clothes and a pair of shoes that Mudiaga would wear on the day of the oral interview. Mr. Zikiye bought a bow tie, a short sleeve shirt, a new pair of trousers and shoes which Mudiaga would wear on the day of the interview. Mr Zikiye who is now the secretary of Ogonbiri elders' forum was optimistic that Mudiaga would be successful at the oral interview.

*****

'When I gave you the name Mudiaga despite your bent leg, I knew you would stand firm one day,' Peregba told his son after he had dressed up for the interview.

'Oh, I nicknamed him Urukpe which means light when he was learning drawing from me,' Mr Zikiye recalled as he and Mudiaga left for Ododo city for the oral interview in Saturn oil company in Ododo city.

'My husband is Prophet Peregba,' Eloho laughed as she admired Mudiaga's clothes and his pair of shoes.

Members of the interview panel had been informed that Mudiaga had been disabled from birth with a bent and twisted leg. They had made up their minds to disqualify Mudiaga on health grounds as a physically disabled candidate.

'Are you sure you're Mudiaga?' Comrade Bamdele asked Mudiaga. 'Mudiaga hired you to come and impersonate him, abi?'

'I'm Mudiaga sir. The native bone doctor treated and straightened my leg after I was involved in an accident.'

He added that the bus he boarded had a head-on collision with Chief Owibo's Prado jeep.
Mr. Bamdele was then convinced.
'Why are you shaking like a barber chair?' another member of the panel who is a white man asked Mudiaga.
'Cold, sir.'
'Oh, how can you survive the winter at the University of Maryland in the United States if you're awarded the scholarship?'
'I will survive sir. I will wear thick clothes that look like a blanket.'
'The three members of the interview panel burst into laughter.
'Such clothes are known as winter jackets. Bush boy,' laughed comrade Bamdele who was drinking his third cup of hot coffee.
Mudiaga realized his blunder. He hadn't worn a sweater and was freezing in the waiting room before he was invited to the conference room where the interview was conducted. When he entered the conference room, it felt even colder, like a deep freeze compared to the waiting room. The three panelists wore coats and ties. The white American official sipped coffee while chain-smoking. The long glass table and silver chairs were the most opulent furniture Mudiaga had ever seen.

Mudiaga presented the three photographs taken during his treatment by the traditional bone doctor. The panel was satisfied he wasn't an imposter.

"Alright, you're dismissed. Check your phone next week for the interview results," Comrade Bamdele instructed.

"My hands and legs are numb!" Mudiaga complained to his sister. "I think my blood is frozen solid."

"I ran out because of the cold too," Ese admitted.

Ese and her brother were discussing the interview when Comrade Bamdele approached and shook Mudiaga's hand.

Comrade Bamdele's phone rang. He answered it.

"Hello, Chief Owibo. Bad news. Mudiaga came to the interview as an able-bodied young man."

"I prefer Mr. Owibo now. The chieftaincy title is irrelevant," Owibo retorted. "So, what happened to Batowei's slot?"

Comrade Bamdele informed Chief Owibo that Batowei never had a slot.

"Mudiaga claimed his rightful place."

Owibo was petrified and speechless. He'd instructed his daughter to abandon her studies, convinced she would claim Mudiaga's scholarship.

"Telling your daughter to drop out was a terrible mistake," Comrade Bamdele said. "It's foolish to empty the water pot at the first rumble of rain. You were trying to collect water with a sieve."

"But Mudiaga was disabled! He had an accident that I thought…" Chief Owibo stammered in self-defense.

He offered assurances that his daughter would try to reinstate her studies. If that failed, she would retake the Joint Admissions and Matriculation Board exams, delaying her education by two years.

"So, Batowei wanted to take my brother's scholarship?" Ese asked Comrade Bamdele rhetorically.

Three weeks later, Mudiaga visited Saturn Oil Company to collect his scholarship award letter.

****

Mudiaga receiving his scholarship award letter from Comrade Bamdele.

Uvo and Mudiaga had gone to fish when Mudiaga heard a beep on his phone. He checked the message and saw that he had won the scholarship. They abandoned their fish hooking expedition and ran home to inform their family members of the good news. The community was agog with joy when the news spread throughout the community. Peregba, his two wives and all the children accompanied Mudiaga to the award ceremony. However, it was only Ese and Uvo that entered the venue of the award. Peregba declined when he was told that only two people could accompany Mudiaga into the conference hall where the ceremony was to take place. Peregba and his two wives agreed that Ese and Uvo should accompany their brother. Ese however recorded the whole event. Following the award ceremony, refreshments were served to the recipients and their families. Eloho, who gave birth to Peregba's daughter six months prior, provided food and drinks for her relatives.

Comrade Bamdele leaned in and whispered to Ese, who was five months pregnant, "You could have had a lot of money if you hadn't rejected me after your school's cultural day three years ago."

Ese simply replied, "We don't value money above all else in our family. Both my mother and my boyfriend are financially secure." She added, "He's an engineer at your oil company, actually." Ese reached into her bag and presented Comrade Bamdele with her traditional wedding invitation, scheduled for two months from then. "Please, come celebrate with me and shower me with the money you claim I missed out on," she said.

"Absolutely not!" Comrade Bamdele snapped back.
"Suit yourself," Ese retorted. "I wouldn't want someone like you, a man who preys on young girls, anywhere near my younger sisters. What's the word, sir?"

'Pedophile,' responded Comrade Bamdele.
'Thank you sir. I don't want a *pidofila* like you to come and harass my three beautiful sisters.'

Comrade Bamdele walked away like a rain drenched chicken Ese then presented Mudiaga with a new phone as a gift from his "small mother" and siblings. Mudiaga was overjoyed.

"Thank you so much, Ese, my dearest sister! When I was younger, you were like a mother to me," Mudiaga exclaimed. "Uvo, you're both my best friend and brother."

"Before the accident, I was a disabled teenager with a limited future," he continued. "But since then, I've become a healthy young man with a bright future. I won this scholarship and I'm going to Maryland!"

"I'll graduate from the University of Maryland as a computer scientist!"

Ese laughed, "Mudi, the poet!" They then revealed the refreshments Eloho had brought after Mudiaga's scholarship announcement.
****

www.ingramcontent.com/pod-product-compliance
Lightning Source LLC
Chambersburg PA
CBHW071758150726
47998CB00005B/1995